'I know you expect preferential treatment as you were here before, but if you look at this,' Laura held out her appointment diary, 'you'll see we've taken on several doctors to replace you and I'm not prepared to allow their lists to suffer in your favour.'

'I see.' The smile which accompanied his reply did not end at Brett's lips. Laura glanced up into his brown eyes and found them filled with appreciative laughter.

'You should lose your temper more often; you've no idea how attractive you are when you're angry.'

Her cheeks flaming, Laura tried to assume an authoritative expression. 'I'm trying to have a serious discussion, Dr Farraday.'

'Yes, Sister Pennington.' Brett tried unsuccessfully to appear contrite. 'I'm deadly serious as well.'

Born in the industrial north, Sheila Danton trained as a Registered General Nurse in London before joining the Air Force nursing service. Her career was interrupted by marriage, three children and a move to the West Country, where she now lives. She soon returned to her chosen career, training and specialising in Occupational Health. Her interest in preventive medicine led to her present work in Health Screening.

Previous Titles

SHARED RESPONSIBILITY
DANGEROUS PRACTICE

BASE PRINCIPLES

BY
SHEILA DANTON

MILLS & BOON LIMITED
ETON HOUSE   18–24 PARADISE ROAD
RICHMOND   SURREY   TW9 1SR

*First published in Great Britain 1991
by Mills & Boon Limited*

© Sheila Danton 1991

*Australian copyright 1991
Philippine copyright 1991
This edition 1991*

ISBN 0 263 77417 1

*Set in 10 on 12 pt Linotron Times
03-9110-51087
Typeset in Great Britain by Centracet, Cambridge
Made and printed in Great Britain*

'If only Marianne could be put in her place so easily,' she murmured, then chided herself for allowing the secretary to get under her skin. Drawing herself up to her full five and a half feet, she strode down the corridor to the furthest consulting-room to check that all was in order. In an attempt to make up for her increasingly frequent doubts about her own place in private medicine, Laura was determined that her standard of work would be, if possible, higher than normal.

'Dressing-gown, patella hammer, sphygmoman-ometer, rectal tray. . .' Not expecting anyone to be around at that time in the morning, she enumerated the items out loud. Hearing the door click, she turned sharply, and was disconcerted to find the lean and wiry shape of a man emerging from the adjoining bathroom, doubly so when she looked up into a pair of laughing brown eyes surmounted by an unruly shock of straight dark hair, cut short in an obvious attempt at control.

'What's this—playing memory games?' The deep velvety tone of his voice held more than a hint of amusement.

'I—er—I—you startled me! I'd no idea there was anyone lurking around. And, come to think of it, what exactly are you doing in there, may I ask? These bathrooms are solely for the use of customers and have already been cleaned in readiness for the morning's clinics. We have enough trouble keeping the rooms of this old building spotless, without you adding to the problem.'

As her halting explanation was followed rapidly by her censure, the brown eyes surveyed her carefully from head to toe. Ignoring her question, he remarked indolently, 'You must be Sister Pennington. I've heard a lot about you. I'm Brett Farraday.'

Laura smiled, relieved by her easygoing introduction to this doctor whom Marianne had incessantly lionised since Laura's arrival in the department. 'Yes, I'm Laura Pennington. Welcome back. I gather you've been away on sabbatical?' And, judging by the way his tropical-weight cream suit set off his suntan, intended that everyone should know it. Especially as spring was still struggling to escape from winter's hold.

'Mm, and returned to find all kinds of changes here. I couldn't believe it when Marianne told me Sister Jones had gone. She seemed part of the establishment when I left a year ago.'

'She seems just as settled in her household routine now, and her baby is due any day.'

'And where did they find you?' The tall angular doctor scathingly repeated his earlier assessment of her trim figure. 'A model agency, perhaps?'

Sensing that he intended the question as an insult to her competence rather than a compliment, Laura felt her cheeks colouring. As his somewhat disparaging scrutiny continued, she revised her first impression of his congenial personality.

'No. I came here as staff nurse eleven months ago, and it seemed just a matter of course when I was promoted.' Unnerved by his glance repeatedly straying to her chest, Laura surreptitiously checked that the buttons of her white uniform were all securely fastened.

'The job wasn't advertised outside the unit, then?'

Resenting the implied criticism of an appointment made two months previously, she tried to demonstrate her total lack of interest by murmuring, 'Not as far as I know. And now if you'll excuse me, Dr Farraday, I have to check the other rooms.'

Her exit from the consulting-room was arrested by his deeply resonant voice commanding, 'Not quite so fast, Sister, if you don't mind—there's a small point I wish to clear up with you.'

'Yes?' Laura assumed a defiant expression as she turned to face him, only to discover him towering menancingly above her.

'About my cancelled appointment this afternoon. I'd like to know what right you had to interfere. Marianne works hard to reel in some of these customers, and I'm not exactly so stacked out with work that we can afford to lose them again.' Pushing back the neatly set out papers on the desk, Dr Farraday perched himself on the edge.

'No, but in my view the lady this afternoon was merely seeking a second opinion on a specific ailment, and that's not what we're here for.'

'It's not? So how *do* you see our role?' His eyes, which now appeared nearer black than brown, held no trace of the earlier laughter. Laura took a step back from their menace.

'We offer health screening to the healthy, discovering pointers to future ill-health. Conditions that have already developed should be referred to a specific consultant.' Determined to get her point over, Laura refused to allow his threatening glower to disconcert her.

'And if their doctor will not refer them? What do they do then?'

Sensing that Brett Farraday would not be happy until

he persuaded her across the thin dividing line between their views, she deliberately widened the argument. 'They have a right to demand a second opinion——'

'Ha, in a perfect world, maybe, but with some of the crusty GPs out there it's not so easy——' His rude interruption was cut short by Laura's retaliation.

'It would be taking money under false pretences if we screened someone who already knew they had a problem. If you referred them on to a private consultant they'd be paying twice, and that's not on.'

Dr Farraday sighed deeply. 'But what I want to know is, how did you become involved with Mrs Kaye, when the appointment was already arranged?'

Guessing his changed attack was tantamount to an admission of defeat, Laura pressed home her advantage. 'The poor woman is nearly demented with worry, and I'm not surprised either. She rang up for more advice and this time was put through to me. It was obvious a health screen wasn't what she needed at the moment, and I told her so. That's all there is to it.' Her spreadeagled hands emphasised the finality of her statement.

'Not so fast, Sister. What's the poor demented lady to do if she's not allowed to see me? Make her condition worse by worrying?'

'She's consulting one of the surgeons next door this morning. I'm sure you'll agree that's better than her wasting any more time.' Laura's voice dripped with condescension as she administered her *coup de grâce*.

'Hrrumph!' As she had expected, he could find no fault in her referral to the outpatient clinic. Laura was sure he would just as readily use the services of the attached private hospital if it suited him. 'Does that mean her GP relented and wrote a referral letter, or is *that* ethical requirement being overlooked?'

'I spoke to the GP, and he was so pleased to learn that we do have scruples, and would not take her money unnecessarily, that he agreed to write a referral letter immediately.'

She watched apprehensively as the scepticism in his look was replaced by resignation, and she was relieved that the outburst she'd expected did not materialise. He merely treated her to a searing look that made her skin tingle, then strode from the room, pausing only to murmur, 'And please accept my apologies for messing up the show bathroom, but I *have* been up most of the night on emergency calls.'

'Phew!' Laura felt as if she had been pulled through a wringer. He had obviously thrown in that last piece of information to make her feel guilty, and, annoyingly, he had succeeded. Checking in the bathroom mirror that her cap had not slipped out of position on her sleek dark bob, she smiled when she saw her reflection. Prepared as she had been for a fight, her cheeks were flushed and her hazel eyes ablaze with anger.

Taking a deep breath in an attempt to regain her composure, she straightened her fringe and continued on her checks of each consulting-room, cursing the inconvenience of the archaic building, but loving the olde-worlde ambience of the high-ceilinged rooms. As she emerged from the last one she was disconcerted to encounter Dr Farraday accompanying Marianne from her office.

'Ah, just the person!' He flashed a warning glance at Marianne as he spoke, and Laura watched her hesitate in the doorway, unsure whether to stay or not.

'How can I help you, Dr Farraday?'

'Brett, please. And may I call you Laura?' he enquired smoothly.

Immediately suspicious of his obsequious approach, Laura nodded guardedly. 'I don't mind, Brett, but the director of the unit doesn't approve, especially in the customers' hearing.'

Brett frowned momentarily, but, obviously recalling that he was trying to appease, he smiled sweetly. 'I think I'm capable of recognising when your professional title should be used, Laura.'

Knowing perfectly well he had something to ask her, Laura checked her watch. 'If there's nothing else then I must get on. The first appointments should arrive any moment.'

'There is something rather important, Laura. Marianne tells me that Dr Andrews has just phoned in sick; she——'

Aghast, Laura broke in, 'Is that correct, Marianne? Why on earth didn't you let me know straight away?'

'That's what I was on my way to do. She asked me to cancel her appointments, but B—— Dr Farraday says he'll take over the list.'

'He can't do that; it's a well woman clinic.' Even if it had not been, Laura would have resented their collusion. Marianne was well aware that her first responsibility was to inform Laura, even though Brett had obviously been in the office when the telephone call came through.

And in the circumstances, he was eager not to lose the opportunity. 'I can surely recognise any problems as well as Dr Andrews——'

'Maybe, but that's not the point.' Laura interrupted

him deliberately, determined he was not going to overrule her. 'Our brochure states that a female doctor conducts these clinics, and Marianne had no right to even suggest——'

'I can assure you that Marianne had nothing to do with it. I overheard the call and immediately offered my services. That's not an insurmountable obstacle, surely?' Brett Farraday had obviously made up his mind and made it clear that he saw no point in arguing further.

'It's an impossibility. The reason most of them come here is that they prefer a female doctor.' Annoyed at being let down at the last minute by Dr Andrews, and not for the first time either, Laura was too angry to wrap her words up tactfully.

'Well, I suggest when the first one arrives, rather than send her away with a bad impression of our organisation, explain the position and ask if she'd mind consulting a male doctor. I'd like to bet she'd rather that than be sent away again after she'd psyched herself up for the examination. Marianne can ring the rest and give them the option of cancelling or seeing me.'

Laura was tempted. Suspicious that Peggy Andrews's excuses were not always truthful, she thought it would serve her right if someone else took over the list.

'But. . .' Laura hesitated, searching for words that would not make matters worse, 'are you happy to undertake these examinations? I mean, these are paying customers. Are you not rusty on the technique?'

Brett's eyes widened at the suggestion. 'What do you think I did as a general practitioner, for goodness' sake? I might have been away for a year, but even if I hadn't visited women's clinics in Africa those kind of skills don't simply disappear.'

'Well, in that case, I suppose it would save our face to a certain extent.' Laura felt herself forced into a corner from which she could see no way out apart from allowing Brett to make himself available. 'But, Marianne, you're not to try and persuade any of the later appointments who might be reluctant to accept a male doctor. Please rebook them for Dr Andrews as soon as possible.'

Marianne glared at Laura and, flouncing back to her desk in the corner of the office, picked up the telephone receiver and dialled the number of the next appointment.

Laura sensed her hostility clearly and guessed Marianne saw Brett's return as a heaven-sent opportunity to defend herself by undermining Laura's position within the screening centre.

The telephone rang at her reception desk, and, pushing her unease over Marianne to the back of her mind, Laura perched on a chair to answer its summons. As she expected, it was the receptionist to warn her that Mrs James, the nine o'clock appointment for Dr Andrews, was on her way through.

Laura welcomed her warmly and asked her to take a seat at the desk while she completed the particulars. Then she took Mrs James along to consulting-room four and closed the door so that she could discuss in private whether she would be willing to consult a male doctor.

Despite Laura's offer to reimburse her travelling expenses, after an initial hesitation Mrs James made up her mind that she would rather see Dr Farraday than return another day. Laura showed her into the adjoining bathroom. 'We'd like you to remove your outer clothes, but keep on your bra and pants and pop on the caftan hanging on the door. And could you provide us with a small specimen in this container?'

'I'll do that gladly. When I'm nervous I always want to go to the loo!'

'Take your time. I'll be back in a few moments.'

Brett was waiting in the corridor. 'Well, what's the verdict?'

'You were right, she has agreed to see you. I'll just check with Marianne about the others——'

'No need, I've already done that, and so far they've all agreed to see me.'

'They have? In that case I should go and have a cup of coffee; you won't have time later.'

Recalling how many times their clients had confided that they came to the Wellstead because they preferred a female doctor, Laura was intrigued to discover whether it was the way Marianne was phrasing the query that was achieving the results.

She waited until Brett was out of the way in the coffee-room at the end of the corridor, then crossed to the office door and stood out of view, listening to Marianne's approach.

'Good morning. Is that Mrs Wells?'

The answer must have been in the affirmative, for Marianne continued almost immediately, 'This is the Wellstead Screening Centre. You have an appointment with us later this morning. I just wanted to warn you that unfortunately our female doctor is indisposed and Dr Brett Farraday is conducting the clinic. I'm sure you'll find him sympathetic and helpful and quite an acceptable substitute.'

Laura moved into Marianne's line of vision for the first time during the conversation, but waited for Marianne to replace the receiver before asking, 'Was Dr Farraday acceptable, then?'

At Marianne's embarrassed nod Laura continued, 'I'm sure he was—you phrased it in such a way that she couldn't refuse.'

Marianne looked sullenly down at her typewriter.

'People expect more consideration from us than that. They're paying for the service and won't appreciate this change at the last minute. If you give me the names and telephone numbers of those you haven't rung as yet, I'll contact them,' said Laura.

Angrily Marianne handed the list over, and Laura took it out to her desk, intending to deal with it after settling Mrs James.

She returned to the consulting-room and, chatting to make her patient feel at ease, she carried out her routine check of weight, height, blood-pressure and pulse-rate, before taking a specimen of blood to check for anaemia. Finally she collected the urine specimen and tested it so that she could enter all the results in the folder of notes before Brett saw the patient.

As she left the room she was pleased to see Alison, her part-time assistant, arriving on duty.

'Oh, good. A male doctor is doing the well woman clinic, so he'll need a chaperon. I'll tell Dr Farraday you're available.'

'But wh——'

'I'll explain later; I've some urgent telephone calls to make.' Laura walked down to the coffee-room and handed Brett the notes. 'Nurse Simpkins is waiting to assist you.'

'I'll call her when I'm ready.'

'She can come in with you now.'

'No way. She'll come when I tell her and not a moment before.'

Laura's eyes widened at the brash finality of the statement. 'I'm sorry, but I must insist. One of the reasons these people pay for consultations here is the uncaring treatment they get elsewhere.' She paused, hoping for his capitulation. When it did not materialise she continued, 'Mrs James is already undressed, and for her peace of mind I insist you have Nurse Simpkins in with you throughout.'

Brett sighed deeply, his eyes darkening with fury. 'For goodness' sake! Anyone would think she's naked. Those caftans provide far more cover for these females than the mini-skirts many of my patients wear to the surgery.' He made his way down the corridor, continuing the argument over his shoulder. 'I'll call your nurse when I'm ready to examine the good lady. I'm not prepared for our initial chat to be inhibited by the presence of a third person.'

Laura knew when she was beaten, and muttered, 'She'll be waiting in the corridor.'

As Brett entered consulting-room four, the telephone rang to inform Laura that his next customer was on her way through.

'I'll take her particulars, Alison, and then perhaps you'd show her to room three. If you're not finished when Brett's ready for help, I'll go.'

'OK.'

Laura had a quick word with Miss Anderson before

handing her over to Alison. She then set about ringing those with appointments later in the day.

She was surprised, but strangely pleased, that despite her different approach only two said they would re-arrange their appointments for when a female doctor was available.

When Alison emerged from the consulting-room with Brett, her eyes were shining. She watched him into the next room, saying, 'Cor, he's dishy, isn't he? Where did you dredge him up from?'

'He's a local doctor, who apparently did quite a bit of screening here before disappearing for a sabbatical year.'

'Where did he spend it?'

'I haven't the foggiest idea—he's not exactly been in a mood for social discussions. Certainly not with me, anyway.'

'But why? What have you done to him?'

'We just got off on the wrong foot. I didn't realise who he was when I found him using one of our bathrooms, and, having torn him off a strip, I was completely wrong-footed when he introduced himself. It's Marianne's fault really. She's gone on about him so much since she heard he was coming back that I was quite in awe of such a paragon.'

'Who could blame her? If I wasn't already married I'd be next in the queue!'

Laura smiled fondly at the heavily pregnant young nurse. 'I think you might change your mind once you get to know him. His personality doesn't match his looks.'

'I don't know about that. His bedside manner in

morning. She closed the notes and handed them back. 'In that case, I can tell you that Phil Munroe has a clinic this morning. If you pop next door quickly you might catch him.'

'Phil? That's great. Should be no problem, then.' Brett obviously knew Phil well enough to have no doubts.

Laura rose from her chair. 'I'll take Mrs Arne a cup of coffee in the meantime.'

'I'd appreciate that.' As Brett strode towards the adjoining hospital, she was rewarded by a grateful smile unexpectedly illuminating his features. She was attempting to disregard the weakness it flashed to her knees when she noticed Alison watching her with interest. Trying to ignore the images of Brett flitting through her mind, Laura nodded towards the clock on the wall. 'It's time you were off duty, Alison. See you tomorrow morning.' Quickly recovering her normal poise, she hastened to collect a tray of coffee and join Mrs Arne for a chat.

'I hope this isn't too strong for you?' Laura poured the coffee into a Willow Pattern cup.

Mrs Arne shook her head, a worried frown marring her attractive face. 'I didn't expect anything like this.'

Laura settled into the chair beside her, and to put her at ease, began to ask about her family.

'I've only one daughter; she's grown up now but lives at home.' Mrs Arne added a sachet of sugar to her coffee.

'Does she work locally?'

'Yes, she's done very well.'

Laura smiled her acknowledgement of Mrs Arne's obvious pride in her only offspring, and was not surprised when Mrs Arne chattered on non-stop in an attempt to ignore the threatening situation.

'She's manageress of one of a chain of boutiques. I think she got her love of clothes from me.'

Laura and Mrs Arne were deep in a discussion of female fashion when Brett returned, and the look of astonishment that crossed his face suggested to Laura that he had not thought her capable of striking up a rapport with his patient.

'I'm pleased to say Mr Munroe is free to come across and see you in a few minutes, Mrs Arne. I'm sure you'll like him—he's one of our best gynaecologists.'

'Thank you very much, Doctor, I really do appreciate what you're doing for me.'

Brett looked abashed and made for the door. 'As you appear to be getting on so well together, I'll leave you with Sister Pennington for the moment.'

Laura watched his retreating back, saddened by the thought that his opinion of her capabilities was obviously not very high.

Mrs Arne grasped Laura's hand. 'Can you stay with me when the consultant comes? I'd feel happier if you would.'

Laura nodded. 'Certainly, as long as he doesn't mind.'

Phil Munroe did not object, and he took his time examining the patient and reassuring her, finally arranging to treat her at the local general hospital at no cost to herself. Emerging at last from the consulting-room, Laura showed Mrs Arne the way out and wished her all the best for her admission to the Westleigh hospital the next day. She returned to find the two doctors deep in conversation. Intending to tidy the

Startled out of her reverie, Laura replaced her cup on the shelf and tried to appear unconcerned. 'I haven't a clue, Dot. This morning was so hectic I didn't have a chance to find out, and I certainly wasn't going to ask him any questions in front of Marianne. When she heard he was returning she no doubt coloured my feelings towards him by implying that he behaved as an ogre towards everyone but herself.'

Dot laughed. 'I think an ogre is the last thing you could call him! He's really very easygoing. It takes a lot to rouse him. Mind, when he does lose his temper you need to watch out.'

'Perhaps his year in the sun has changed him; he's lost his cool a couple of times already today.' Although Laura joked about their differences, she couldn't help remembering how Brett had charmed everyone else— a thought that led her to wonder if he was only reacting to her own prickly behaviour.

Their tea-break was disturbed by the telephone pealing, and as Laura crossed to answer it, she was disconcerted to see Brett and Marianne returning from the dining-room, both their faces alight with laughter. Obviously her absence had been the catalyst their interrupted friendship required.

Any benevolent feelings she might have been experiencing evaporated rapidly. Snatching up the receiver, she snapped into the mouthpiece, 'Yes?' Hearing that the first afternoon appointment was on her way through, she asked Dot to deal with her in room three. Then, grabbing her diary, she marched down the corridor and asked Brett if she could have a word with him in room four.

'Certainly. How can I help you?' Amiably he followed her in and closed the door behind them.

'I want to know how often you intend to work here. Our rooms are pretty solidly booked——'

'Oh, yes, I know. I've checked with Marianne when there are free spaces and she'll book lists for me at those times.'

Laura took a deep breath, clenching her fists to try and hold back the outburst that was welling up inside her.

'You may have done that, Dr Farraday, but I only arrange nursing cover for the sessions *I* know about. Any others would have to be cancelled for lack of staff.'

'But——'

'No buts, Dr Farraday. I know you expect preferential treatment as you were here before, but if you look at this,' Laura held out her appointment diary, 'you'll see we've taken on several doctors to replace you, and I'm not prepared to allow their lists to suffer in your favour, whatever Marianne may think.'

'I see.' The smile which accompanied his reply did not end at his lips. Laura glanced up into his brown eyes and found them filled with appreciative laughter.

'You should lose your temper more often; you've no idea how attractive you are when you're angry.'

Her cheeks flaming, Laura tried to assume an authoritative expression. 'I'm trying to have a serious discussion, Dr Farraday.'

'Yes, Sister Pennington.' Brett tried unsuccesfully to appear contrite. 'I'm deadly serious as well.'

Exasperated, Laura exclaimed, 'Which sessions have you arranged for this week?'

'Only today and Thursday morning. I do have other commitments.'

'I was going to ask you about that. Are you rejoining the Westleigh Health Centre practice?' Turning the diary to Thursday's page, Laura scrawled Brett's name across the top.

'Yes. But only on a part-time basis.' His voice assumed a flippant tone as he added, 'I'm hoping to fill the remainder of the week in other ways.'

'Such as?'

'Ah, that's a very good question.' Brett touched the side of his nose with a fingertip, making Laura regret her probing.

Surreptitiously studying the cut of his clothing and his expensive leather shoes, she tried unsuccessfully to suppress the suspicion hovering at the back of her mind. If Brett obviously had no urgency to find regular work, he must have a more than adequate private income.

In an attempt to return to safer ground, and hoping to prompt him into revealing something more about himself, she asked, 'Where did you go for your sabbatical, Brett?'

'Africa—S-Sudan.' Obviously startled by her change of subject, Brett stumbled over his reply.

'With one of the voluntary organisations?'

'A very small missionary society. Why?'

Laura's suspicion that finding work was not of prime importance to him was strengthened with every word he spoke, although she had to admit she found the fact difficult to reconcile with his spending his sabbatical year in the Sudan. That certainly indicated an unsuspected commitment to hard work. She was beginning to find him something of an enigma and was intrigued to know more, but she could hold up the afternoon clinic no longer.

'No reason, I just—well, wondered where you'd got that tan. However, Nurse Griffiths should have your first patient ready by now, so we'd better finish this discussion later. In the meantime I'll arrange to cover your Thursday session this week.' Closing the diary firmly, Laura opened the door.

Looking baffled by her sudden appeasement, Brett made his way into the next consulting-room and got the afternoon session under way.

Seeing Dot replace the telephone receiver, Laura enquired, 'All well?'

'Mrs Black, Brett's next customer, on her way through,' Dot consulted the list on the desk. 'Looks like his last, if the others have cancelled.'

'Yes, a quiet afternoon. Convenient, really, as I want to see the director if possible.' Laura lifted the folder of notes from the desk. 'I'll deal with this one, so can you chaperon Brett when he's ready?'

Dot nodded. 'My pleasure.'

Carrying out the routine checks on Mrs Black, Laura conversed automatically, allowing her thoughts to stray to Brett. She suspected he would not tolerate delay when it was his suggestion at stake and guessed he would be looking for an answer to his colposcopy query before the afternoon was out. Although what it had to do with him she didn't know. It was really the gynae-cologist's problem.

'I'm just going to take a small blood sample. Rest your arm on here, would you?' Laura placed a pillow under Mrs Black's elbow.

As she waited for the vein to engorge sufficiently, her thought returned to colposcopy. She must get all the pros and cons straight in her mind before confronting Mr Edwards, the unit director.

'Right, I think that's all for now.' Laura handed Mrs Black a couple of magazines to peruse. 'Would you like a cup of tea or coffee?'

'Coffee would be great, thanks. No milk or sugar.'

When Laura took in the tray, she checked that Mrs Black was warm enough, and reassured her that Dr Farraday would not be long.

The moment Dot emerged from room three, Laura took the opportunity to slip next door to the hospital, where she knew the storeman would lend her an equipment catalogue. She returned to her desk and totted up the cost of the colposcope together with the special couch and chair, not to mention the specific instruments. The total was horrific, especially when she had not included any treatment machines.

As Dot finished chaperoning Mrs Black at that moment, Laura called her over. 'I'm leaving you in charge. I'm off to see if Mr Edwards is free, so you know where I'll be if there's an emergency.'

'Problems?' Dot's eyebrows were raised in hopeful anticipation of some gossip.

'It's not a problem, just the gynae men want to set up a colposcopy unit here because there's no room next door.' Laura shrugged. 'I'm not sure if it'll be a good thing or not, but I want to get my say in first.'

'It'd make our work more interesting, wouldn't it?'

'But that's not the only consideration. The cost of the equipment is pretty exorbitant—look at this total!' Laura proffered her calculations to Dot. 'We'd have to charge pretty stiffly to get back that outlay. *And* it would take a room out of use. I know we don't use five all that often, but it's useful when we get a backlog.'

Ten minutes later, Laura found herself defending Brett's idea in the face of Mr Edwards's blunt refusal to even consider the project.

'We're purely a screening centre.' He leaned forward, placing the tips of his fingers together. 'The place for a treatment service is next door, probably in Outpatients.'

'Perhaps my description hasn't exactly done it justice. You see, initially it is a screening process. When a patient has an abnormal smear result, the only way to know whether treatment is necessary is to have a closer look. That's colposcopy.' She paused, hoping Mr Edwards would accept her defence, before she tentatively mentioned that it was just a bonus that the colposcope could be used to assist in the treatment of milder cases.

'I still think it would be better sited in the Outpatients department.'

'But they've no room——'

'Or they give that excuse. Perhaps they've looked into these figures——' he picked up Laura's papers contemptuously '—and don't consider it a cost-effective proposal.'

Laura sighed. 'It's a pity, really, but I guess you're right. I must confess I came to see you armed with similar arguments against the idea, but I felt I had to turn devil's advocate.' As the director perused her figures once more she continued, 'At least you'll be prepared when Mr Munroe approaches you himself.'

Mr Edwards smiled. 'You'd better leave me all those

figures—I might need them for ammunition.' He studied Laura's calculations for a moment. 'This is the
absolute total cost, is it?'

'No, that doesn't include treatment facilities. Not
knowing whether laser treatment or coagulation would
be Mr Munroe's choice, I left that out. There's such a
vast price difference between the two machines.'

'The lasers being dearer, no doubt.'

Laura nodded. 'And don't forget we'd quite likely
need another member of staff on duty to cover the
unit. That would bump up the cost still further.'

Mr Edwards compressed his lips. 'Hm. What gave
Mr Munroe the idea, do you think? He doesn't usually
come into the screening side, does he?'

'No. Dr Farraday asked him to look at one of his
screening patients——'

'Brett's back, is he?' Mr Edwards frowned. 'But
surely he doesn't screen the females?'

Quickly Laura explained what had happened that
morning 'I thought it better to have an alternative to
offer rather than just turn them away.'

'Good thinking. But if Brett's involved, it won't
finish here. He can be quite persistent. I think I'd
better have a word with the hospital director about
this. Leave it with me for the moment.'

Laura returned to her department feeling she had
done her best both for the department and for the
proposal. It was not her decision now. She could safely
leave that in Mr Edwards's hands.

Brett did not agree. 'Well? Is it all decided?' he
asked the moment she walked into the coffee-room
where he and Dot were reminiscing.

Laura shook her head. 'Mr Edwards doesn't think it's a good idea, I'm afraid. He——'

'Was no doubt persuaded by you,' Brett broke in rudely to finish the sentence incorrectly.

Laura took a deep breath and counted slowly to five. 'If that's what you want to believe, fine.' Intending to say no more, she was about to walk away when she found the temptation to correct his assumptions irresistible. 'However, if you'd like to know what really happened, Mr Edwards was so uncompromising that I found myself defending your scheme——'

'Good girl, I'm pleased to hear it. I did get you wrong, didn't I?' As he interrupted her, Brett's features assumed a self-satisfied expression that left Laura unsure whether he was more pleased with his discovery or with himself.

'Not entirely. I have to admit the defence was against my better judgement.' As she started to tidy her desk another thought struck her. 'I don't see why you're becoming so involved, though. It's surely a matter for the gynae men?'

'Mm, but I have my reasons.'

'Which are?' Laura was intrigued.

'Ah, that I'm not prepared to divulge at the moment.' Leaving Laura angry with herself for asking, Brett took his leave informally and made his way down to Marianne's office.

Laura watched them leave the building together, and could not help thinking that really they deserved one another. But in that case, whey did the sight of them together leave her feeling so disconsolate?

CHAPTER THREE

LAURA was about to begin the Tuesday afternoon screening session when she saw Brett hovering at the door of consulting-room five.

Recalling that she had only agreed to him working Thursday, she handed the lists she was checking to Dot. 'Hold the fort here a moment, while I see what Dr Farraday wants.'

She strode down the corridor, mentally preparing what she would say if Marianne had booked a list for him without informing Laura.

However, she greeted him cordially, almost too sweetly. 'Can I help you, Dr Farraday?'

'Ah, Sister Pennington, good to see you. This room isn't in use today, is it?' Brett pushed open the door a fraction, then, having satisfied himself it was empty, turned to Laura with a smile.

'No. Why?' she enquired coldly. 'Are you intending to consult here?'

'Nothing like that, I understood you only too well yesterday and will be in Thursday morning for my next session.' He hastily closed the door again.

Annoyed by his reference to her assertiveness of the previous day, Laura felt a flush spreading up to the roots of her hair as he continued, 'No, I just wondered if Mr Munroe and I could look around and perhaps take a few measurements.' Laura noticed for the first time the tape-measure balanced on his clipboard of papers.

She frowned. 'For what reason? I told you Mr Edwards was against your ideas for the colposcopy unit.'

'Mm, but that doesn't mean we're prepared to accept his decision. We have an appointment with him at three.' Brett checked his watch as he spoke.

Sorry not to be able to answer otherwise, Laura admitted that the room was not booked.

'Thanks. I needn't delay you any longer, then, Sister.' Having noticed Mr Munroe striding along the corridor, Brett beckoned to him, then opened the door of room five, standing back to allow Phil Munroe to precede him into the room.

Despite Brett's dismissal, Laura stood her ground in the doorway and eavesdropped on their plans, many of which she was not happy about. If they succeeded in changing Mr Edwards's mind, their ideas would leave her with no overflow consulting-room. Even before she had suggested the scheme to Mr Edwards, Laura had worked out how the room could be utilised for both if necessary.

'I hope you don't mind if I butt in.' She moved further into the room, causing Brett to turn around sharply, his look plainly stating that it was a private discussion.

'Go ahead, Sister.' Laura was grateful for the gynaecologist's encouragement in the face of Brett's hostility.

'Your ideas for the colposcopy unit to be sited here would mean our department losing a consulting-room.' Ignoring Brett, Laura addressed her remarks to Phil Munroe. 'Don't you think it would be better to at least make the room dual-purpose, so that it can be used for consultations when not in use by you?' Noting Phil's obvious interest, she pressed home her advantage. 'These rooms are so enormous, I'm sure it's a feasible proposition.'

Mr Munroe smiled. 'It sounds a sensible idea, Sister, and ought to appeal to the powers that be. How do you think we should go about it?' He lifted Brett's clipboard and turned to a clean sheet of paper.

Laura gave them a rough idea of her perceived layout, including the conversion of the colposcopy couch for routine examinations.

'You've made some very good points there.' Phil Munroe was busily scribbling the whole time she was talking.

Brett remained silent, which suggested to Laura that he wasn't exactly pleased at her usurping his position as the consultant's adviser. He looked pointedly at his watch, prompting Mr Munroe to enquire, 'Are we getting late for our meeting with the director?'

'Not yet, but I think we ought to sketch something out before seeing him. Is your office free?'

Laura had things to do herself, and, having had her say, did not object to Brett's attempt to monopolise the consultant and exclude her from any further discussion. But she wasn't going to let him have all his own way.

Bestowing an ingratiating smile on Mr Munroe, she murmured, 'Please use this consulting-room. I'll close the door behind me and see you're not disturbed.'

She did just that, knowing by the look on the consultant's face that he at least was grateful for her intervention. If Brett wanted a battle he could have one! Especially now she had made it clear to Phil that not only was she not out to wreck their plans, but she would co-operate wherever possible.

She was clearing up at the end of the afternoon when she spotted Brett entering Marianne's office. Although she longed to know how the meeting had gone, she was determined not to ask. As she tidied consulting-room three, Laura overheard Marianne saying dolefully, 'I can't tonight, Brett. I've far too much to do here.'

Knowing another unpunctual start to the day had put Marianne way behind with her work, Laura could not help but think the secretary had only herself to blame. Unwilling to listen further to Marianne's whining attempt to gain Brett's sympathy, she moved away to sort out the coffee-room. She was banging cups and saucers together so noisily that she did not hear Brett coming up behind her.

'That coffee smells good. Is there enough left in the pot for a small cup?'

Laura shrugged. 'Plenty. But I should think it's pretty stewed by now.'

'That'll be all right, it's the caffeine I need.'

'Late night last night, then?' she taunted.

'No, early morning, in fact. I was called out about three-thirty, so it's been a very long day. However, I shall feel quite differently when I've sunk this.' Brett drained the cup and piled it on the tray with all the others. 'Don't you want to know how our meeting went?'

Remembering the reason for his using the bathroom the previous day, Laura was conscious that she had jumped to a mistaken conclusion about his nocturnal habits for the second time. In an attempt to make amends she nodded grudgingly. 'If you want to tell me.'

Brett shook his head. 'I don't know what I've done to deserve this icy treatment, but perhaps you'd care to enlighten me over dinner this evening. You see, we ought to celebrate victory for the colposcopy idea.'

'Victory?' Laura was astounded. 'You mean—you mean Mr Edwards——'

'Has capitulated.' Brett could contain his enthusiasm no longer. 'A chance directive from head office helped, but he was finally swayed by your ideas, so I'd like you to celebrate with me.'

'My ideas? What do you mean?' Watching Brett rather than what she was doing, Laura absentmindedly turned the tap on full, causing the force of the water to strike the coffee jug she was washing and splash back into her face.

Trying to suppress his amusement, Brett handed her a paper towel from the holder on the wall.

'Mr Edwards didn't want to lose a consulting-room, but when we gave him your suggestions it made all the difference.' He rested a hand on her shoulder, half turning her towards him. 'And to think I suspected you of trying to hinder our plans rather than help! So what do you say, my raven-haired beauty?' His brown eyes searched her face relentlessly. 'Is it a date?'

Laura was so overwhelmed by his attributing the success to her that she nearly accepted, until she recalled Marianne's obvious refusal of his invitation not ten minutes earlier. She had no intention of being second choice.

'I'm sorry, I've other plans.' She knew her answer

must sound stilted, but she'd never been good at telling lies.

'So I'm not forgiven for whatever it is I'm supposed to have done. Ah, well, perhaps another night.' Brett regarded her steadily for a few moments, then, turning on his heel left the department without another word.

For one brief moment the feeling of loss Laura experienced at his departure made her want to call him back and agree to go out with him after all. Instead she turned her attention to getting off duty as quickly as possible, trying to convince herself that she had had a lucky escape. Despite the antagonism between them, she could not deny feeling drawn towards Brett and would almost certainly have agreed, if she had not overheard his earlier conversation with Marianne. And if he had only invited her because he was at a loose end, she would surely have lived to regret it.

It was not until the next afternoon that she learnt all the details of Mr Edwards's decision. Phil Munroe came to tell her that he had operated that morning on Mrs Arne and thought he had caught the tumour in the nick of time. There appeared to be no spread to other abdominal organs.

'I'm so pleased, Phil. Will she need any radiotherapy?'

'Just prophylactically.' Hesitating briefly, he added, 'You know, Brett Farraday is a very good diagnostician. That's not the first time he's picked up something that might easily have been missed. I hope we might work together more if this colposcopy plan comes off.'

Suspicious that he was singing Brett's praises for her benefit, Laura ignored his remarks about Brett, asking instead, 'How did the meeting go yesterday?' She hoped to learn more details if she feigned ignorance of the outcome.

'It went very well. As you so rightly said, Mr Edwards was against the idea, but once we discovered his main objection was the loss of a screening-room we were able to change his mind with your suggestions.' Phil Munroe rubbed his hands together gleefully. 'My, Brett was more than pleased at our success. Didn't he take you out to celebrate? He said he owed it to you.'

'No. Er—I had other plans for the evening,' Laura replied thoughtfully.

'Ah, well, he'll probably make up for it another night.'

As Phil made his way through to the adjoining hospital, he left Laura wrapped in thought. Had she in fact misjudged Brett the previous evening? After all, she had only heard Marianne's reply. Brett could have been asking something entirely different. Despite their obvious friendship, Dot discounted its being anything more. But if Brett had mentioned Laura to Phil in his first rush of enthusiasm, why had he only asked her out after first approaching Marianne? If Brett liked to play the field in that way, his presence in the department would do nothing to improve the working relationship between Marianne and herself.

Laura returned to her parents' home that evening in a pensive mood. Although it wasn't exactly what she had trained for, she enjoyed being in charge of the department and found the work challenging enough to hold her interest. However, if she was unable to defuse the tension Brett was creating she was sure her skills could be better utilised elsewhere. The snag was finding suitable employment that allowed her to assist her parents each evening. The Wellstead was a convenient distance from home, and while it might require her to start early each weekday she did have every evening off.

She would have felt happier if the preventive screening service had been available for all, instead of just the privileged few who could afford it. True, some firms sent their employees along for health checks, but they were few and far between, and all too often it was only the senior management who were offered the perk.

However, if abnormal smears could be followed up at an affordable price, that would certainly help to redress the balance. As she helped her father up the stairs to bed, she came to the conclusion that the colposcopy unit was a scheme that deserved her support—a decision that sent a warm contentment flowing through her veins at the thought of working harmoniously with Brett rather than against him.

Next morning she set out for the Wellstead feeling more settled than she had for the past couple of weeks, and even admitted to herself that she was not averse to the thought of Brett Farraday's holding a clinic that morning.

He was already in the department when she arrived on duty at eight. Seated at Marianne's empty desk, he was reading through a couple of sheets of paper.

'Good morning, Dr Farraday. You're an early bird and no mistake! Your first appointment isn't for three-quarters of an hour.' Eager to make amends for her earlier aloofness, Laura greeted him warmly, but Brett seemed not to notice.

'I know. I came in to check the report Marianne has

typed for me.' Without even looking up, he picked another couple of sheets from the desk. 'It sets out our official proposals and I want to circulate it as soon as possible. Now we've a tentative go-ahead, I can get on with the plans.'

Laura shrugged. 'I'll leave you to it, then,' and started on her morning routine.

'Just a minute, Laura.' Shuffling the papers together, he followed her into the corridor. 'I meant it when I said we ought to celebrate the other day. The offer still holds. How about tonight?'

Remembering her conversation with Phil, Laura was aware that there was nothing she would like better, and as long as she remembered it was only his way of thanking her she could see no harm in joining him. 'That sounds great. I'd love to. Thanks, Brett.'

Attempting to hide his surprise at her unexpected agreement, Brett smiled down into her eyes and said, 'Good. I'll pick you up about eight. Where do you live?'

As she was about to tell him, Laura noticed Marianne coming towards them, her ears straining to catch their conversation even before she reached them.

'I'll let you have it later, Brett.' Laura dived into consulting-room four before the fact that she was going for a meal with Brett became the latest departmental gossip.

Brett must have followed Marianne into her office, for when Laura emerged their heads were bent over the papers he had been studying earlier. Laura tried to ignore the stab of uncertainty that assailed her at the sight, telling herself it was her he had asked out after all.

His clinic ran without any problems, until his last consultation was finished and Marianne handed him the results of Monday's tests.

'Damn, come and look at this,' Brett ordered as Laura was tidying the room. 'This was the second lady on Monday. Her smear is reported as being consistent with moderate to severe dysplasia, and there's not a thing I can do about it unless we get this unit set up.' He looked distressed at the thought of his helplessness.

'Are there no other units in the area that you could refer her to?'

'Only one, and she could wait six months for that.'

'Even when it could be severe? Surely she'd be classed as an emergency?'

'Not an emergency exactly, but it does want looking into pretty promptly. Is her phone number there? I'd better have a chat with her.'

As Laura watched Brett dialling the number she mentally commiserated with him. Her concern for his dilemma served only to confirm her decision to support the new unit.

He joined her at lunch in the staff canteen, and, after briefly explaining how upset his patient had been, continued, 'Let's hope we can offer the service here sooner rather than later, making this situation a thing of the past. We'll have another one next week. The last lassie on Monday turned up an abnormal one as well, but she's away at the moment.'

'I still don't understand why you're so involved, Brett.' Recalling his snub earlier in the week, Laura added tentatively, 'Surely it's the gynae department's problem?'

'Yes and no. Having discovered an abnormal smear,

we're the ones left to persuade the patient that the delay in obtaining treatment is no risk. Not an easy task.'

'No, I can imagine how I would feel if I couldn't get treatment immediately.'

Brett looked up in surprise. 'Even though you knew there was no risk in the delay?'

Laura's cheeks coloured at his reaction to her admission. 'It's psychological, isn't it? The big C looms large in all our minds. I suppose we're conditioned into an irrational fear of it.'

'It's the advertisements for cervical screening that are at fault. We need a campaign to inform people that an abnormal smear is only an indication of a pre-cancerous state.' Brett helped himself to a glass of water. 'But no one will provide the money for that, you can be sure.'

'No, I guess not, so I suppose it's up to us to educate, especially those who can't afford our service.' Laura pushed aside her dinner plate and started to peel an orange. 'As long as the charges aren't out of everyone's reach, the sooner you start the colposcopy unit the better.'

'Oh, I've got a convert now, have I?' Brett laughed delightedly. 'Is that due to my stirring up your personal feelings?'

Embarrassed, Laura wished she could escape back to her department, but she was blocked into her corner by the pathology staff, who were just starting their main course.

'Probably. However, I *am* surprised at Phil Munroe leaving the planning to you. Surely he's in a better position to know what's required for the unit?'

Attempting to divert his attention, Laura returned to her original attack.

Brett cleared his plate and helped them both to a cup of coffee from the machine.

'He probably does. But I have the advantage of time at the moment. He's up to his eyes in work——'

'So will he have time to use the new unit?'

'It'll probably be in the evenings to start with, which won't be easy for your staff cover, but I'm hoping to talk him into allowing me to do some during the day. It would be another source of income.'

Laura drained her cup and prepared to leave the table. 'That's the attraction, is it? That's what all this boils down to—money. You really aren't thinking of all these poor ladies worrying for months on end—you just see colposcopy as a means to line your pocket.' Annoyed at herself for being taken in, Laura left the dining area and made for the stairs back to her department. Brett soon caught up with her, and, taking her arm, swung her to face him.

He did not speak immediately, but treated her to a long, hard look with narrowed eyes. Laura felt like a laboratory specimen under his scrutiny.

'Correct me if I'm wrong,' he said at length, 'but, on very short acquaintance, I'd say you have an obsession about money—or perhaps about the lack of it.' Allowing her to pull free from his grasp, he watched her for a moment longer. 'Do you think you're in the right place, if you feel this way?'

Laura coloured hotly, annoyed that she had allowed her uncertainty about private medicine to show so plainly, but if she had over-reacted it was not without good reason. It was her response to the weeks spent watching her father's suffering. Knowing the increasing pain could be relieved immediately by a hip replacement, she thought she was probably failing him in some way by cosseting the wealthy healthy who came to the Wellstead clinic for regular check-ups.

'I've been asking myself the same question. I enjoy my work, but——'

'But you think it's immoral, is that it? I came back from Africa feeling the same way, but I soon came to realise that there are many different ways of life, and the best way to help those at the bottom of the pile is to exploit those at the top, if you see what I mean.'

They arrived back in the screening department as he finished speaking and were greeted by Dot.

Reluctant to incriminate herself further by the wrong answer, Laura welcomed the interruption. If only she had kept her comments bottled up! She regretted antagonising him more than she cared to admit, for she was usually the first to realise there was no way the present set-up could be altered. Life was unfair, and if she couldn't accept that the sooner she changed her job, the better.

Much to her relief, Brett appeared soon to forget her outburst, for before leaving the department he reminded her about their date that evening.

Laura was surprised, and a little apprehensive when she was summoned to Mr Edwards's office later in the afternoon, especially when she discovered that Brett had been there earlier.

'Dr Farraday wants us to obtain the colposcopy equipment yesterday at the latest! I think it would be a good idea if you could visit the suppliers tomorrow and see what's available.'

'I've only a small clinic in the afternoon. I could go over then.'

'Why don't you do that, and take a requisition form with you so that you can get the order under way? Perhaps Dr Farraday would accompany you.'

'Oh—er, yes, I suppose it would be sensible to take someone who's done colposcopy before. I suppose he has?'

Mr Edwards nodded. 'Not regularly, but he's not a novice.'

Remembering her evening outing with Brett, Laura made up her mind to ask him then about the next day. Just in case he would not be free she would take the catalogue with her, and he could suggest what he thought would be the most suitable equipment for their purpose.

When five o'clock came, she made her way to her parents' home in a contented frame of mind.

She helped prepare a meal for her mother and father, then left them to eat it while she showered and washed her hair in readiness for Brett's arrival.

Wanting to look her best, she wore a simple suit of cream shantung that was the most expensive item in her wardrobe. At least she wouldn't feel she was letting him down.

When it got to eight-thirty, she began to wonder if she could possibly have mistaken the night or even the time he had stated, but by nine she knew she was fooling herself making allowances for him. He had probably decided after their chat at lunchtime that he didn't want to go out with her. She had just climbed the stairs to change back into jeans and a sweater when her mother answered the telephone.

'It's for you, dear,' she called up the stairs. 'Brett somebody or other.'

Laura stomped down into the hall, intending to give him a piece of her mind, but he only gave her the chance to thunder, 'What——?' before interrupting.

'I'm sorry, Laura, I never expected there to be a problem this evening as I wasn't on call, but just before six I was called urgently to Greenfields and have been there ever since coping with a psychiatric emergency. It's taken me all this time to get him certified and removed to a psychiatric hospital where he can do himself no harm.'

'Oh—er—I see.' Laura swallowed repeatedly in an attempt to regain her composure. 'I must admit I was wondering what had happened to you.'

'Would you still like to go out and eat, or shall we celebrate another night?'

'Oh, I think it would be better if we left it for tonight. You must be absolutely shattered.'

'I am, but I don't like to let you down.'

'Don't worry about it, Brett. But about the reason for our celebration—I've got the go-ahead to visit the medical suppliers tomorrow afternoon and I wondered if you'd be interested in seeing what's on offer.'

'Great. What time will you be going?'

'Three-ish, if that's all right by you.'

'I'll pick you up at the hospital, and perhaps we could rearrange our date for tomorrow evening?'

Laura agreed, and almost immediately regretted doing so in case it gave him the idea that her social life was not very active.

However, she was waiting for him promptly at three the next afternoon. Having changed out of her uniform into jeans and a white sweatshirt, she wondered if she ought to have made more of an effort when she saw him striding towards her in his dark suit.

'I must just have a quick word with Marianne,' he murmured as he swept past her down the corridor.

Laura followed slowly, accepting that Brett probably had letters to sign from the day before. However, as she reached the office she heard him say. 'And what about the ones I gave you last night? Are they ready?'

Marianne shook her head. 'No. If you want them to go off today, you'll have to come back later.' Marianne's gaze slid across to Laura, taking in the fact that she was out of uniform and apparently waiting for Brett.

But Laura could give Marianne's obvious enmity no further thought. She was too busy trying to work out what Marianne meant by 'last night'. Had Brett spun her a tale when in reality he had found the time to visit Marianne? Laura knew only too well that making excuses was easy for doctors. An emergency could always conveniently crop up. And it seemed that Brett Farraday was a dab hand at smooth-talking his way out of trouble. She had certainly been taken in, a fact that annoyed her much more than his breaking their date.

CHAPTER FOUR

BRETT caught up with Laura as she hurried along the corridor in an attempt to evade Marianne's prying gaze. In one hand he was clutching a copy of the rough plan he had circulated to everyone interested in the unit, and, obviously aware that something was wrong, grasped her shoulder firmly with his free hand.

'Let's get out of here, then we can chat in peace.'

Laura found herself being propelled through the front door as she almost ran to keep up with his angry stride.

He did not speak until he reached his car and unlocked the doors, and then it was only to order, 'Jump in.'

Laura surveyed the interior of the Mercedes and wished she had gone to the equipment suppliers alone. She felt uncomfortable in the face of such incontrovertible luxury.

As the car pulled smoothly away from its park, Brett turned to Laura. 'Now, why the return of the Ice Age after yesterday's thaw?'

To give herself time to gather her wits, Laura murmured, 'I don't know what you mean.'

'Oh, I think you do. Why did you walk off? Something upset you, and I want to know what.'

Conscious that the last thing she could tell him was the truth, Laura felt the colour rising in her cheeks as she answered, 'I was only being polite. Even though I might not always see eye to eye with Marianne, the last thing I wanted was for either of you to think I was eavesdropping.'

'Marianne is an extremely competent secretary.' Brett's concentration on the road ahead did not waver.

Glancing at his profile, Laura guessed his irrelevant reply was intended to prompt her to say more. She gave her next words careful consideration.

'I have no complaints about her secretarial ability when she's there. It's her unexpected absences and unpunctuality that I find so difficult. Like this morning. I'm on my own until Alison arrives at nine, and I couldn't get on with my own work for answering her phone.'

Brett raised his eyebrows non-committally as he swung the car into Meditec's car park.

'I'm sure it doesn't happen as frequently as you're trying to make out. You know what the trouble is with you, Laura. You expect everybody to do everything by the book, and your book allows not even the slightest deviation to take account of human frailties. I don't suppose it ever occurs to you that people might have problems outside the Wellstead's walls.' Climbing from the car, Brett slammed the driver's door with more force than was necessary.

Aware that he had no idea of her own home circumstances, Laura bit back the defensive retort that sprang to her lips—an instinctive response for which she was more than grateful when he behaved as if the previous conversation had not taken place.

Opening the passenger door, he asked, 'Have you the catalogue and order form?'

Laura nodded as he helped her from the car.

However, his next words cut short her relief.

'We'll continue this discussion later. For the moment we'd better concentrate on choosing the best equipment.'

She had to admit that Brett certainly knew exactly what he wanted and intended to get it at a price beneficial to the Wellstead. The salesman must have sensed he was fighting a losing battle, but nevertheless made a last valiant attempt.

'You must realise, Dr Farraday, that this equipment has been developed to a high standard——'

'I'm aware of that,' Brett interrupted, 'and for that reason I'd prefer to buy yours. However, if the price is not right we'll have to look further afield.'

The salesman gave in and began to work out the smallest discount he thought he could get away with. When Brett refused to accept the first figure, but pressed for a bigger reduction, Laura was more than grateful that he had accompanied her. She was not sure she would ever have withstood the browbeating.

A firm order was placed and early delivery arranged before they left the premises.

'Great!' Brett exclaimed as they drove from the car park. 'We'll soon be in business if they fulfil their promises.' He checked the time. 'We've been longer than I expected. It's way past six, and Phil asked us round for a drink this evening to report on our shopping expedition. He'll be expecting us before long. Is that all right?'

Laura nodded. 'But I can't go dressed like this.'

'Why not? It's only a quick informal chat. I'm going to change into something more casual.'

'But I'm wearing jeans——'

'So what? I expect Phil will be too.'

Laura gave up trying to make him see it as a problem and accepted that he was probably right in what he said.

'OK if I nip home and change, then?'

Again Laura nodded, then voiced the question that was still niggling away in her subconscious.

'Brett, why really are you prepared to devote so much time to finding the right equipment for Phil's unit?'

No doubt recalling her accusations of the previous day, he appeared to consider his choice of words carefully. 'The other day when I called Phil Munroe in to see Mrs Arne, I took the opportunity to sound him out about a clinical assistantship in Gynae. He seemed quite keen.'

Laura regarded him thoughtfully.

'So it's in your interest to get the unit under way as soon as possible?'

'Well, it is a project I'd like to see developed promptly, but I can assure you the urgency is solely for the welfare of those who would otherwise have a long wait for colposcopy.'

'I'm glad to hear it.' Relieved that he appeared to have forgotten their earlier discord, Laura acknowledged that she might have been a little hasty in her judgement of Brett.

After a short drive from the industrial side of town, Brett slowed down as he approached the downs. Whatever she might have imagined, Laura was totally unprepared for her first sight of what she could only call a mansion as he swung the car into the long curving drive.

'This is home?' she gasped, her eyes wide as she took in the mammoth proportions of the grey stone building.

'Not exactly mine. I have a flat on the other side of the downs. This is the parental pile, but at the moment I seem to spend more time here than at the flat. I'm sorry Mum and Dad aren't home to meet you, but they're just coming to the end of a month in Bermuda. I'm caretaking.'

'Oh, I see.' Laura felt completely out of her depth and allowed herself to be led through a cavernous front hall into an elegant sitting-room decorated in a style that must have been all the rage when the Victorian house was built.

'What can I get you to drink?' Brett crossed to the window where a tray of bottles and glasses sat upon a dark ornate circular pedestal table.

'Dry sherry, please.' It wasn't exactly her favourite drink, but, having noted the small selection of bottles, she guessed it would be a safe choice.

Brett poured himself a shot of whisky and wished her the best of health.

After he had taken a couple of sips he enquired, 'How hungry are you?'

Unsure why he was asking, but not having stopped for lunch, Laura murmured, 'So-so. I can wait a while.'

'Would you like to eat out, or shall I get Mrs Mates to rustle us something up here when we get back from Phil's?'

Laura knew she should have realised that to run a house of that size would need help, and the servants were obviously on call. 'Surely it would be unfair to ask that without any warning?'

Brett regarded her steadily over the rim of his glass. 'You really do regard me as an out-and-out reprobate, don't you? I can assure you that our kitchen has every conceivable mod con. As well as large freezers we have microwaves and ovens that ensure it doesn't take long for a meal to be ready for the table. In fact, we've moved right out of the Victorian era of *Upstairs, Downstairs*.'

Acutely aware that her ingenuous perception of the situation deserved his raillery, Laura longed to escape from a situation she was finding difficult to handle. However, rather than risk further embarrassment by appearing over-eager to leave, she attempted to divert the conversation.

'I'm not exactly dressed for dinner. Perhaps it would be better to leave it for another evening.'

Brett raised his right eyebrow sceptically. 'Afraid of being alone with the big bad wolf, is that it?'

Her cheeks flaming, Laura inwardly cursed her stupidity in leaving herself open to his teasing. However, he spared her any further torture by adding, 'I'll change into jeans too and we'll go where they're acceptable. OK?'

Laura nodded, and when Brett had drained his glass he left the room, saying, 'Won't be a minute, help yourself to another sherry if you'd like one.'

However, she was so busy drinking in the beauty of the finely proportioned room that he was back before she even gave the amber liquid in her glass another thought.

'The carving on these chairs is magnificent, Brett. I've never seen anything like it before.'

'No, more's the pity. But, even if the craftsmen were

still around and able to spend so much time on one chair, the present level of wages would price the work way beyond reach. Come on, let's go. Phil will be wondering where we are.' Taking Laura's arm, he pulled her towards him, tucking her hand securely in his pocket. Then without any warning, he tipped her face upwards and kissed her as if it was the most natural thing in the world that he should.

Although he released her immediately, he maintained his grip on her arm. The fluidity of his every movement emphasised his composure in sharp contrast to his earth-shattering effect on Laura. Though she was sorry not to see any other parts of the house, she was relieved that her trembling legs had only to negotiate the length of the hall. It took the chill of the evening air to return her senses to normal after Brett's assault on them.

Stealing a quick glance at the man by her side, she was disappointed to see total unconcern on his face, as if the kiss had meant nothing to him.

But what else could she expect? she asked herself. Just thinking of the difference between that one room and her parents' tiny council house was sufficient to make her realise the tremendous disparity in their lifestyles. Recalling his rapport with Marianne, she guessed the secretary probably came from a similar circle of friends, hence his wangling her the job. Perhaps he had planned this visit to the house to see how Laura would react. If so, her behaviour had probably fallen short of what he expected.

In that case, the sooner she got this thank-you meal out of the way and returned their relationship to a business footing, the better.

As Brett helped her into his car she attempted to disregard the spark his touch ignited within her and asked, 'Where does Phil live?'

'Just along the road from here, towards the town.'

He did not speak again until he had parked the car in Phil's drive.

'Right, out you get. Let's give Phil the good news.'

Laura felt happier with the conversation reverting to business topics. 'Shall I bring the catalogues?'

'That's a good idea, then we can show him exactly what's on order.'

'Hi, Laura, Brett.' Phil welcomed them warmly, and Laura was amused to notice he *was* wearing jeans as Brett had predicted. 'This is Kim, Laura. She's been trying unsuccessfully to persuade the twins to go to sleep.'

Brett, who obviously knew Kim well, kissed her warmly on the cheek and turning to Laura nodded to the stairs. 'Go and peep, they're the most adorable pair of ruffians.'

Grinning proudly, Kim led the way. 'He only thinks that because he's their godfather.' She lifted a finger to her lips as she gently pushed open the door.

From the silence, Laura guessed Kim had been more successful than Phil had predicted. She looked past the proud mother to see two fair-haired cherubs, each sucking a thumb as he slept.

'They are gorgeous. How old are they?' Laura whispered as Kim silently closed the door.

'Nearly three.'

'Both boys?'

'Yes, Alistair and Brett, named after their god-fathers. I expect you've already noticed how Brett loves children.'

Laura was about to say there had been no opportunity when Kim continued, 'It makes all the difference to a relationship.'

Laura suddenly realised what she was hinting at. 'Oh. We only work together.' The last thing she wanted was for Kim to get the wrong idea. 'Brett isn't. . .' Her voice trailed away as she noted the scepticism in Kim's face.

'But I thought you were on your way out for a meal.'

'We are. It's Brett's way of thanking me for my support over the new unit.' As they rejoined the men, Laura realised the futility of her argument. Kim clearly preferred to stick with her own beliefs.

'I've shown Phil the order.' Brett handed Laura the catalogue. 'He thinks we've done very well. He——'

'Just curb your enthusiasm for a moment while I get these ladies a drink.' Phil cut short Brett's eulogising to settle Laura and Kim with the Martinis they both requested.

After further discussion about the proposed unit, Brett suggested it was time he and Laura left.

'Wouldn't you like another drink first?' Phil was on his feet and collecting their empty glasses.

'No, thanks, Phil—I'm driving. And, as I've booked a table, we ought to be going.' Brett was already on the way to the door.

'Thanks again, Laura. I'll see you next week.' Phil winked conspiratorially, as Kim said, 'Next time you must get Brett to bring you when the twins are awake.'

Feeling distinctly uncomfortable, Laura thanked them both for their hospitality, and heaved a sigh of relief when Brett helped her into the car. She waited for his angry reaction to Kim's last remark; certain he must suspect the girls of gossiping. So when it did not materialise she hoped it meant he had not heard.

As they turned on to the road again, she stole a glance at his profile and seeing no sign of recrimination asked, 'Where are we going?'

'A little bistro with a cosmopolitan menu. It doesn't look very pretentious, but the food is out of this world.'

'Sounds unusual.'

Her first sight of the menu confirmed that she was going to enjoy the meal, and they eventually agreed on a seafood pasta starter, followed by guinea-fowl cooked in Calvados. Obviously amused at her delight in the varied choice, Brett ordered a bottle of white Bordeaux to accompany the main dish. Laura was pleased that their chat touched only on general topics, at least until they had finished the food.

'Now, tell me something about yourself. Have you always lived in Westleigh?'

Laura nodded. 'Born and bred here, and trained at Westleigh hospital.'

'And you still live at home?'

'Yes.' She remembered that her mother had answered the phone to Brett the previous evening, and, eager to dispel any wrong ideas he might be harbouring, she rushed on, 'I'd like to move away, but my mother needs help looking after Dad. That's why I looked for a job with most evenings off.'

Brett gave a small gasp. 'Your father is an invalid?'

'Not exactly. He has arthritic hips and is waiting for surgery. He sits around so much he's getting rather overweight, so Mum find him difficult to manage, especially in and out of bed.'

Brett rubbed his brow thoughtfully. 'I'm sorry,

Laura.' Taking her hand, he massaged her palm with his thumb, obviously trying to convince her of his sincerity. 'I was a bit insensitive earlier, wasn't I? But I can assure you I had no idea——'

'I realise that, Brett.' Embarrassed, Laura just wanted to change the subject. 'Don't worry about it.'

'But I do worry. It must make socialising difficult.'

'Mum and Dad are very considerate. If I'm going out they work around me. Dad'll wait up until I get home tonight.'

'I see.' Brett was thoughtful. 'So what do you do with your spare time?'

'Luckily I'm an avid reader, so I can do that at home. Not so easy are trips to the theatre, but I manage usually one visit a month.'

'Who do you go with?'

Feeling he was probing deeper than she was prepared to allow, Laura shrugged. 'Just depends. It varies.'

Brett obviously sensed that he was invading her privacy and changed the subject. 'What do you think of the local rep?'

'Usually very good. Do you go?'

'Sometimes. When I'm not on call.'

'Your family are obviously local. Where did you train?'

'I didn't go very far—Southampton.'

'The medical school there has a good reputation.' Laura would like to have discovered more about his private life, but instead they went on to discuss the relative merits of some of the local hospitals. Before they knew it, the restaurant was waiting to close.

Leaving the car park, Brett set off to drive towards Laura's part of town. Knowing he would insist on escorting her right home, she could not help but wonder what he would think of it compared to his parents' lavish abode.

As he turned into her road, Laura felt suddenly unwilling to find out. 'You can drop me here, Brett.'

He braked suddenly.

'Where's your house?'

'Just along a bit—here will be all right, though. The road narrows and you might not be able to stop outside.'

Brett's face registered surprise mingled with disbelief. 'I can pause briefly, surely, and I can assure you I intend to see you safely indoors.'

Laura sighed resignedly. She should have realised that he would not find any other course of action acceptable. 'Thanks. That's number twenty-three—on the corner.'

Brett stopped the car for a second time, surprisingly showing little interest in the building she had indicated.

'We must do this again, but I'm on call for the remainder of the weekend. Perhaps we could go to the theatre some time?'

Guessing his vagueness indicated a reluctance to commit himself, Laura merely said, 'Goodnight, Brett, and thanks.'

As he leaned across intending to kiss her, she turned and opened the Mercedes door, running up the front path before he had a chance to follow.

'And that's that,' she told herself as she helped her father to bed. Much as she had enjoyed the meal Brett had felt duty bound to offer, she hoped she had now made clear to him that there was no necessity to repeat the invitation. Even though she could not help but admit to a few pangs of regret. Despite all her reservations, she had felt comfortable in his company. Smiling, she realised that she too was now a convert to his flock of admirers!

Laura's weekend was spent helping her parents with the routine shopping and housework, and attempting to make life for her father a little more comfortable.

'We'd like to go to church, Laura,' her mother said on Sunday morning, 'but I really don't feel I can cope with your father alone. How about coming with us and helping?'

Laura, who had got out of the way of churchgoing when she started her nursing training, agreed half-heartedly. However, she found the experience so moving that as the final hymn was announced she flashed a smile of gratitude to her mother for asking her.

At that moment a muffled bleep sounded and Laura turned her head in time to see Brett slipping out of the back pew and through the door.

She could not have explained why, but the knowledge that they had shared the service sent a warm glow through her.

However, as she helped her parents from the church, she bumped into Marianne, wearing what Laura could only describe as a supercilious expression, and all her fine feelings evaporated as the suspicion grew that Marianne had been with Brett at the back of the church.

Laura returned to work on Monday morning to find Marianne absent again, and foresaw a difficult day ahead. However, the secretary arrived only a quarter of an hour late, and Laura was pleasantly surprised by

her application to her work until she had caught up
with all that was outstanding. Brett had no appointments, and the morning ran smoothly. When he arrived
for his afternoon list, everything was ready.

'Three this week,' he joked. 'Things are looking up,
and as they're all men I shan't need a chaperon.'

Laura smiled, despite the veiled rebuke she felt he
was administering. 'That's good, because we'll be busy
elsewhere.'

And, good as her word, she kept right out of his
way, allowing Dot to prepare his patients for him, but
nothing more. Peggy Andrews's list was a full one and
the women waiting for her attention were always ready
to confide their worries and ask for advice. Laura
enjoyed her afternoon, knowing that the health edu-
cation she offered was not wasted on unwilling
recipients.

As she left the last one safely ensconced with Peggy,
Laura noticed Brett watching her every move from the
coffee-room. Ignoring him, she took her seat at the
desk in the corridor and began to sort out the day's
paperwork. Brett sauntered over.

'Busy day?'

Laura bent her head lower over her books in an
attempt to prevent the colour flooding into her cheeks
and giving away her innermost thoughts. 'Busy
enough.' She had intended to demonstrate her indifference by ignoring Brett, but the mixed emotions fer-
menting within let her down.

'Then how about relaxing over a quiet meal this
evening? Your choice this time.'

Laura couldn't believe her ears. Surely Marianne
would have told him Laura had seen them at church?

Did he expect to win her co-operation by asking her out when he had nothing better to do? Did he consider himself so irresistible that she would not mind? His bare-faced audacity resulted in a sharp intake of breath from Laura before she could trust herself to speak.

'No, thank you, Dr Farraday. I must get home.'

'In that case, can I give you a lift? Save you waiting about for buses in this torrential rain.'

'It's very kind of you, but I won't be ready to leave for some time yet.' Laura attempted to total the clinic figures for the day, but with Brett remaining so close the piquancy of his masculinity assailing her senses prevented her concentrating. She sighed and closed the book, intending to move away from his disrupting influence, but he laid a hand on her shoulder, and when she looked up to discover the reason, she could not miss the look of total bafflement that clouded his face.

'Did you not enjoy yourself on Friday?'

'I thought it was great, thank you. I also appreciated your help at Meditec, but that's all. Now, I'm sorry, but I have work to do.'

Ignoring the air of disbelief that replaced Brett's initial bewilderment, Laura moved into the first consulting-room and started to change the linen ready for the morning.

When about half an hour later she saw him stride down the corridor and out of the department, she tried to ease her pangs of disappointment by telling herself that his abrupt departure proved her right. Whatever her feelings might be, Brett saw her as nothing more than a colleague whose co-operation was vital to his plans. It would only have increased the heartache he was already inflicting if she had accepted his invitation.

[faded text from previous page bleeding through, illegible]

CHAPTER FIVE

HE COULDN'T have been gone for more than ten minutes when Peggy Andrews came out with a worried look on her face.

'Dr Farraday gone?' she queried.

At Laura's nod she grimaced. 'Blast! He saw this girlie last week when I was away. Her smear result is abnormal, but she's leaving next week to teach English to the Zambians and her contract is for a year. Is there any way we can get her colposcoped before that?'

'We can arrange a private appointment with one of the gynae men easily enough, but although we have equipment on order there are no private facilities available at the moment.' Puzzled, Laura continued, 'Hasn't Brett contacted the girl already?'

'He probably tried, but she's been in Paris since Wednesday and rang from the airport in the hope of speaking to one of us about her results.'

'Oh, yes, I remember him saying she was away. Phil Munroe was very helpful to Brett last week—perhaps if you ring him? He's the one who suggested setting up the unit.'

Phil was busy in the operating theatre and could not be disturbed, so Peggy said she would contact him later and let Laura know the outcome the next day.

So she was surprised when, a couple of hours later, Brett telephoned her at home. 'Hi, Laura, sorry to disturb you, but I wondered if there was any news from Meditec. Have they suggested a delivery date yet?'

'No, I haven't heard anything. Why——?'

'If I can persuade Meditec to let us have our order, or even borrow the necessary equipment, can Phil and I use it tomorrow afternoon? Only one patient, but necessary.'

Laura thought briefly. Dot would be on duty, so there was sufficient nursing cover. 'It's for the girl going to Zambia, I presume. It'll be all right as far as I'm concerned, but what about the engineering department? They have to OK all equipment before it's put into service.'

'I'll get on to Meditec first thing. In the meantime, how about joining me for a drink to discuss the details?'

After a moment's thought, Laura agreed. Having got her father to bed safely, it seemed to her an ideal opportunity to learn more about a procedure she knew nothing about, especially if they were starting the unit the next day.

The moment she replaced the receiver she regretted the impulse that had made her accept. As she donned a black skirt that was smart rather than fashionable, and added a white top to emphasise her dark colouring, she couldn't help but wonder if for some reason Brett was checking up to see if she had gone straight home.

However, by the time he arrived to collect her, Laura had convinced herself that the invitation was nothing more than another example of Brett's impatience to have everything done yesterday. So, rather than have her mother jump to the wrong conclusions, Laura slipped out of the house almost before Brett's car was stationary.

He welcomed her with a broad smile as he assisted her into the passenger-seat. 'Where to?' he asked.

'I—I don't mind.' The heady combination of his warm greeting and his overt masculinity prevented her brain coming into focus.

Brett seemed not to notice. 'Right, we'll make for the Trout. It's about the nearest.'

As he set the car in motion Laura studied his profile guardedly. He wasn't exactly handsome, but there was no denying the powerful vibes he emitted.

As if he sensed her gaze on him, he turned to meet her eyes and with a lift of his right eyebrow enquired. 'You don't think I'm all bad, then?'

Sure he had read her mind, Laura felt the heat rushing to her cheeks. As she tried to hide her confusion she heard Brett chuckle, making her silently vow to ignore his sardonic comments in the future.

However, he immediately confounded the thought by saying, 'Seriously, I see this as an opportunity to get to know you better. We do seem to have had our wires crossed, and I thought perhaps if we uncrossed them we might even find we like one another.'

Knowing she didn't need to uncross any wires to do that, Laura kept her head averted to prevent him seeing just how must she cared already. Mistakenly thinking it was his declaration that had caused her high colour, Brett laid a warm hand over hers and squeezing it gently said, 'I can see you feel the same, so let's forgive and forget, eh?'

Realising that a more harmonious working relationship would be to her advantage, Laura nodded while stifling the retort that sprang to her lips. To hide her amusement at his egotism, she pretended a keen interest in his skilful parking of the car.

The lounge-bar was full, but after Brett had succeeded in attracting the attention of the barman long enough to secure their drinks, they managed to squeeze into a couple of wall seats at a corner table. Conscious that the elderly couple opposite could hear every word, Laura found conversation difficult.

So she agreed with relief when, draining his glass, Brett raised his eyes to meet hers and said, 'This isn't the best place, is it?'

He was already rising from his seat, and Laura followed him. As they walked across the car park he draped his arm loosely around her shoulders, causing her step to falter.

Apparently unaware of the effect he was having on her, Brett began to chat about the colposcopy procedure.

Suddenly conscious of her silence, he turned her towards him. 'I'm not maligning you, am I? You don't know more about this business than I do?'

At Laura's confession that she knew very little about the subject, Brett brightened. 'I've got a book at home that explains it clearly.'

. 'Perhaps I could borrow it tomorrow?'

Brett was now so fired with enthusiasm for the project that tomorrow would not do. 'I'd rather you read it before we do our first case. I'll get it for you on the way home.'

Laura wondered when he thought she was going to have time to read it, but decided it was best not to argue. Expecting the book to be at his flat, she was surprised when he turned into the drive of his parents' home.

'I'll wait here, shall I?' Intimidated again by the size of the house, Laura made the tentative offer as he brought the car to a halt.

'Of course not. You can meet Mum and Dad. That's if they're in, which is beginning to look unlikely.'

Laura allowed herself to be propelled along the drive, and as Brett swung open the front door she sensed immediately that they were alone in the building.

'Come and see the library. You didn't have time for a conducted tour on your last visit.'

Laura was pleasantly surprised to discover that the library was a homely room with a coal fire burning low in the grate. If it hadn't been for the book-lined walls, it could have been the sitting-room of her own home.

'Drink?' Brett had already removed a couple of glasses from the corner cupboard.

'Would coffee be too much trouble?'

'Of course not.' He lifted a book from the shelf by the door. 'This is the one about colposcopy—you can peruse it while I'm doing the chores.'

Instantly contrite at being difficult, Laura offered, 'Can I help?'

Brett appeared about to refuse, then he laid the book on the coffee-table and, taking her hand, pulled her to her feet. 'Of course, you'd like to see the kitchen where we keep the servants tied to the table leg.'

Determined this time not to rise to his bait, Laura answered in the same vein. 'Only if you're sure they don't bite.'

He laughed delightedly as he led her through a long

passage to the back of the house. 'I knew once you allowed yourself to relax that sense of humour would be lurking.'

As they entered the spacious kitchen, Laura saw he had been right. It housed every labour-saving device imaginable.

'Perked or instant?' Brett was already filling the kettle.

'Instant's fine.' Laura watched as he spooned coffee into china mugs. 'I bet even I could produce something edible in this kitchen.'

'I'll take you up on that. You can come and cook me a meal some time.' He moved closer, resting his hands on the wall on either side of her.

Laura shrank back against the work surface, hoping he didn't think she had been angling for an invitation.

'Oh—er—I didn't mean. . .' She broke off in utter confusion as she became aware of the heat radiating from his body.

Brett's answering chuckle was almost a caress. 'You're a timid little fawn, still shying away from me.' He leant over and kissed her lips so gently that she thought she might have imagined it. 'Come on, back to the library and we can chat in comfort.'

As she was about to seat herself in the armchair by the fire, he murmured, 'Don't be so aloof; come and join me on the settee.'

Reluctantly she did as he asked, and immediately regretted it. The moment she placed her mug of coffee on the table, Brett took her in his arms and rained spine-tingling kisses over every inch of her face. Kisses that excited a response from Laura's body that she was sure was most unwise.

He took her attempt to move away as encouragement and pulled her even closer, kissing her so thoroughly that she could do nothing but abandon herself to her emotions.

As all reasoning flew from her mind, she felt unable to prevent her hands sliding round to the back of his neck and tangling in his hair.

When he eventually released her, he held her slightly away from him and surveyed her affectionately before saying, 'There, that marks a definite improvement in our relationship, doesn't it, Sister Pennington?'

The spell broken by Brett's use of her professional title, reminding her that it was nothing more than her co-operation at work he was interested in, Laura angrily pulled away from his grasp. She lifted her mug from the table and moved as far away from him as she could.

'Don't shut me out now, Laura. Not now we've found there *are* things we like about each other.'

Angry with herself for being taken in by his plausibility, Laura snapped, 'We were talking about working together, nothing more.'

Brett raised his eyebrows and shrugged. 'OK, if that's the way you want it.'

'It is. And, if you don't mind, I'd like to go home, Brett. I'm supposed to start work at eight, and with Marianne being so unreliable I try to get there earlier.'

'What for?' Brett's tone was scathing. 'So you can catch her out?'

Laura was incensed. 'Of course not, but if the lists aren't ready the clinics start late. I'm afraid if it continues I'll have to report her to Mr Edwards.'

Brett sat up straight, his eyes blazing. 'That would

be an underhand thing to do! Has it never occurred to you that there might be a good reason for her absence? Why not say something to the girl herself?'

Laura hadn't intended provoking him into a defence of the secretary, but he was certainly making it clear whose side he was on. 'As it happens, I have—several times,' she told him, 'and have been met with insolence.'

'Insolence? Oh, come on——'

'It's true.' Laura was determined he would hear her out now. 'She hints that there's a problem at home, but refuses to say what it is——'

'And you can't accept that?' Brett had risen and was towering above her menacingly, making Laura feel she must justify herself.

'No. Not when it disrupts the running of my clinic——'

'Your clinic?' Brett interrupted, even angrier than he had been earlier. 'Delusions of grandeur now, is it? I know you enjoy being the big boss, but, really, that's going a bit too far!'

Taken aback by his vitriolic attack, Laura started to protest, but he silenced her by raising his hand warningly.

'No, you listen to me. If Marianne does arrive late she tries to make up for it by working in the evening, or by working through her lunch-hour.'

'And no doubt she has a good reason for that too,' countered Laura, remembering Brett's frequent visits to Marianne's office.

'And what do you mean by that?' he demanded coldly.

Laura had no intention of answering and instead

reiterated her earlier demand. 'I'd like to go home now, please, Brett. Especially if you expect me to read this book before tomorrow.' Laura was determined to prove *her* commitment to work could not be questioned.

'Right, I'll run you back.' Brett now appeared more saddened than angry, and his easy compliance took Laura by surprise. Throughout the journey home she watched his expression change from anger to bafflement, but after his earlier put-down there was no way she was going to attempt to redeem the situation.

As she thanked him and took her leave, he seemed about to say something, then, apparently dismissing it as hopeless, said he would see her the next morning about the equipment.

Determined not to be caught unprepared, Laura stayed up into the early hours reading the book he had lent her. When she tried to sleep her brain was too active, and, recalling the feelings he had stirred up within her, she felt saddened that the only partnership he was looking for was a working one.

Laura rose exhausted from her restless night. but relieved that at least Brett would not be able to fault her on her knowledge of colposcopy. However, the next morning it soon transpired that he was not going to get his own way.

'They haven't some of the equipment in stock, so we'll just have to wait.'

'When does the girl actually leave?' Laura riffled through her pile of folders, hoping Brett would take the hint that she was too busy to stop and talk.

'Not until a week on Friday, but we were allowing time for two visits in case she needs treatment.'

Laura's distracted nod could have left him in no doubt that the conversation was closed, and she was not surprised to see him meandering into the office for a chat with Marianne. She was disturbed by his presence and hoped she had seen the last of him for the day. However, within minutes he came to find her again.

'Marianne tells me you're arranging a farewell meal for Alison on Friday. Aren't I invited?' Brett appeared hurt by the omission. 'I'd like to add my good wishes.'

Reluctantly Laura said he would be welcome. 'We haven't decided where as yet. I'll let you know on Thursday.'

'Are you collecting for a present?'

At Laura's nod Brett handed over a more than generous contribution, saying, 'Is that all right?'

She nodded. 'That'll be a great help. Thanks.'

Throughout the next couple of days she puzzled over her resentment of Brett's intrusion on their female night out. After all, they had invited Mike Thoms, so it was only because he was otherwise engaged that Peggy Andrews was to be the sole representative of the medical staff.

The longer she thought about it, the more Laura had to admit that Marianne was the cause of her misgivings. Brett had already made too much of an impact on Laura's life for her to appreciate his openly aligning himself on Marianne's side for the whole evening.

Dreading Friday's celebration, Laura spent most of Thursday wondering if there was any way out of her dilemma, but all the time she knew that as she was sister in charge there was no way she could duck out of it.

Hoping to buy the present during Thursday's late-night shopping, she kept her fingers crossed that the lists would not overrun their allotted time. She was delighted when they finished promptly, allowing her to get away early.

'Rushing off?' Hastily tidying her desk, Laura was far from pleased to hear Brett's familiar voice.

'Yes. I want to get Alison's leaving present, something for the baby.'

'Is it likely to be heavy? I'll come with you and pick it up in the car if you like.'

Laura would rather have gone on her own, but knew it would be downright churlish to say so.

'It shouldn't be too heavy. I'm looking for a baby alarm, so if you know anything about electronics it'd be a help.' She hesitated before saying tentatively, 'That's if you're sure I'm not keeping you from anything important?'

Brett regarded her keenly before shaking his head. 'I wouldn't have asked in that case.'

Conscious of his reproach, Laura murmured, 'I'll just nip down and change out of uniform.' She arrived back to find Brett ensconced with Marianne in the office.

'Right, I'll see you tomorrow, Marianne. I'm looking forward to it.' He added for Laura's benefit, 'Marianne tells me you've booked a table at Hansards. I've been meaning to try it ever since it opened.'

'Mr Edwards recommended it, so I hope his taste is good. That reminds me, did you hear any more about the colposcopy equipment?'

'Not a word. I'll try and ring them again tomorrow.'

'Let me know if you have any success, won't you?'

Laura found what she was looking for in the Mothercare shop, and, as there was some money left, said she would like to spend it on Alison. Not knowing what Alison would like, she settled on a gift token from Boots, saying she would stipulate that it had to be spent on Alison herself!

'Good idea,' Brett agreed as they walked to his car. 'Now how about giving yourself some consideration and joining me for something to eat?' When he saw Laura shaking her head he went on, 'Or even a drink?'

'I'm sorry, Brett, I have to get home—Mum expects me.'

'Parental obligation again?'

Laura treated Brett's question as rhetorical, wishing there was some way she could make him understand she didn't see it as a problem. They were a united family and she wanted to help. However, he did not refer to the subject again as he drove her home, and she felt unable to broach the subject as he chatted about his trip to Sudan and his work in the Westleigh practice.

'I'll keep the present in the car—and take it straight to Hansards. Would you like me to wrap it? I can get the paper at the newsagents.'

Caught unawares by his offer, Laura nodded. 'That would be great.'

She knew the expression must sound trite, but she was worried by Brett's display of amiability. The hostility between Marianne and herself would make the evening at Hansards difficult enough without his trying to avoid demonstrating a partiality to either of them.

As Brett escorted her from the car, he offered to drive her to the restaurant the following evening.

Laura's immediate thoughts of Marianne were answered as if he had read her mind.

'I'm picking Marianne up at the Wellstead, then going on for Dot, so it won't be out of my way.'

'In that case I'd be delighted. What kind of time?'

'I should be at your house about seven.'

'Fine.' Laura hurriedly inserted her key in the lock. 'Thanks for your help, Brett. See you tomorrow.'

Brett had obviously not expected such a perfunctory dismissal, and Laura's determination to keep their relationship on a business footing began to waver, until she recalled his blatant support for Marianne the previous evening and quickly let herself into the house.

'Supper's ready, dear,' her mother greeted her, and Laura reluctantly pushed her worries about Brett to the back of her mind, and threw herself into the evening routine.

It wasn't until she was in bed that she allowed thoughts of him to return to the fore. However, even with time to go over every possibility, she found Brett difficult to fathom. He seemed determined to impress her with his charm and helpfulness. And, though she had to admit that he was everything she had ever admired in a man, she was convinced that his conviviality was solely in the interest of more co-operation at work—a fact that Laura found doubly frustrating when she was already trying to prove her efficiency as head of the department, he still thought more of the feckless Marianne. Switching off the bedroom light, she drifted into a dreamless sleep.

Friday at the Wellstead was busy, erasing all thoughts of Brett from her mind until she was on the way home. As she hadn't heard anything from him about the colposcopy equipment, she assumed he had had no luck with Meditec.

After helping her mother with the usual evening chores, Laura changed into a powder-blue soft jersey dress with a draped neckline, and slung a black jacket over her shoulders. It was an outfit she had had for a couple of years, and she always felt comfortable yet smart in it.

As she watched for Brett's arrival she berated herself for dressing up for him despite her rejection of his friendly overtures. She knew in her heart of hearts that if he hadn't been joining them she would probably have gone to Alison's send-off in jeans.

The moment his car drew up, Laura called her farewells and slipped out of the front door before he could reach it.

'Hi. You look a different person from the hard Sister Pennington tonight. Much softer somehow.' He took her arm, squeezing it lightly. 'Must be the dress. It suits you.'

'Thanks,' murmured Laura briefly, trying to will any trace of colour from her cheeks. Marianne's eagle-eyed presence in the passenger-seat would soon detect any hint of embarrassment, and Laura wanted a happy evening for Alison.

They arrived at Hansards to find that Peggy Andrews and Alison had not arrived, so they settled in the bar and Brett bought a round of drinks.

As he handed Laura her glass of Martini and lemonade, she heard him swear softly, and looked up to see him smiling towards a foursome just entering Hansards.

'What are you doing here?' he queried, surprising

Laura with his abrupt tone. 'You said you were eating at home.'

'Now don't get agitated.' The middle-aged matron with the blue rinse laid a placatory hand on his arm. 'The Perrys rang and asked us out at the last minute. We had no idea they were bringing us here.'

'You'd better take a seat and I'll get you all a drink.' Brett's tone was resigned. 'This is Laura, the screening sister, and Dot, one of the staff nurses. You know Marianne, of course. This is my mother,' adding as an unnecessary afterthought, 'and Mr and Mrs Perry.'

As Brett looked around, Mrs Farraday told him her husband was already buying their drinks.

Brett seated himself sheepishly between Marianne and Laura, and did not join in the ensuing conversation until Peggy and Alison joined them. As he ordered their drinks, the waiter informed him that the table was ready for the Wellstead party, so Brett suggested they move into the restaurant right away.

As if determined to show no favouritism, he again sandwiched himself between Marianne and Laura, leaving the others to find seats where they preferred.

After the order was given, Laura turned to Brett. 'You didn't seem particularly pleased to see your parents.'

'No, I was rather taciturn, wasn't I?' Laura was relieved to note that Brett appeared shamed by her accusation. 'But that's one of the penalties of practising in my home town. I know Mum and Dad move in the same social circles, but just occasionally I feel our frequent encounters are not exactly coincidental.'

Laura smiled. 'The fact that you've remained within

easy striking distance of home must mean you accept their interest.'

'Interest I don't mind, but Mum wants a grandchild and is hounding me to get married as soon as possible.'

Too embarrassed to know how to reply, Laura fell silent, and, having accepted her whitebait starter from the waiter, turned her attention to her other neighbour, Alison.

As the only male present, Brett was presented with the wine-list, and they all agreed to leave the choice to him. As the majority were tempted by steak dishes, Brett picked out an Australian red.

'Australian?' Laura was intrigued enough to turn to him with her query.

'The quality of some of their wines surpasses many French vintages. The problem is knowing which ones, but I'm confident you'll all enjoy this Cabernet Sauvignon.'

He was right. In fact, they all enjoyed the meal so much that at eleven they were still lingering over coffee. However, Alison was tired and intimated that she wanted to get home.

'Just one moment, then.' Brett slipped out to his car and brought in the beautifully wrapped present. Making a short speech, he ended by wishing her an uneventful pregnancy. 'And we look forward to seeing your healthy son or daughter when it arrives.'

Delighted with her presents, Alison thanked them for the happy time she had spent at the Wellstead. Before she and Peggy left, they asked about their contribution to the bill.

'It's all taken care of,' Brett told her.

'But. . .'

'But nothing. I've seen to it, and that's the end of it.'
And he would not entertain another word on the
subject. Guessing he had paid the bill on his way out
to fetch the gift, Laura found his reluctance to flaunt
his action unexpectedly touching.

Although she was not working the next day, she was
pleased when they left soon after Alison. She had
found it an exhausting week, and the sooner she was
away from Brett's disturbing influence the better, for,
despite her resolution, she had to admit an increasing
difficulty in hiding her feelings for him.

Expecting to be delivered home before the others,
Laura became apprehensive when Brett dropped first
Marianne and then Dot, leaving them alone in the car
together.

When he invited her into the front seat Marianne
had vacated, she felt tongue-tied and uncomfortable.
To break the silence she mentioned his father, who was
such a bluff and hearty man, that he would always be
the life and soul of any gathering. 'He was talking
about his business interests. They sound pretty varied.'

'They are now, but he made most of his money from
the family building firm started by my grandfather. He
just happened to be in the right place at the right time.'

'Is he still involved with building?'

Brett turned to smile at her. 'Yes—why the interest?'

'I thought perhaps having made his money he would
have sold out.'

'I've told you before, people are seldom as mercen-
ary as you seem to expect. Knight and Day is a family
firm. It means a lot to him even though I——'

Not listening to his last words, Laura interrupted

You have to be approved to carry out any extended role afresh when you move jobs, otherwise should a problem arise you won't be covered.'

Brett's first patient arrived at that moment, so Laura demonstrated what needed to be done for the males and handed him over to Brett.

'We don't get much of a break. Dr Andrews's next patient will be here any moment, and some Mondays we have Dr Thoms here as well.' Laura rejoined Pam, who was labelling the blood bottles. 'Mr Grant didn't need an electrocardiogram, but if they come for an executive health screen that's our job as well.' Leading the way into consulting-room two, she removed the cover from an impressive computerised ECG machine.

'You'll soon get the hang of this, Pam. It produces the trace without our help apart from fixing the electrodes to the patient.' She lifted a packet of self-adhesive pads from the lower shelf of the trolley. 'We use these, and you can't really go wrong, as their positions are clearly marked on this diagram etched into the surface.'

Pam carefully inspected the equipment before asking, 'Do any of the men require one this morning?'

Laura consulted the list. 'Yes, as a matter of fact the next one does—Mr Abbott. I'll try and do that when you're free to watch.' As she finished speaking, she lifted the receiver from the telephone that had been clamouring for her attention. 'Sister Pennington here. Can I help you?' After listening briefly to the caller, she turned to Pam. 'That's Peggy Andrews's next patient. If we deal with her together, we should both be free when Mr Abbott arrives.'

Laura's assumption was correct, so they both followed Mr Abbott into room two when he arrived. 'Don't be intimidated by so much attention,' joked Laura. 'As it's her first day in the unit, Nurse Rainer's just learning the routine.'

'I don't mind at all, in fact I quite welcome the idea of two attractive nurses dancing attendance on me.'

Laura carried out the routine checks before asking Mr Abbott to remove his shirt, socks and shoes.

'Have you had an ECG before?'

'No.'

'Right, well, I'll ask you to hop up on to the couch now and make yourself comfortable. Then we attach you to this machine—and I promise you won't feel a thing until we peel the stickers off your hairy chest at the end!'

'Sounds delightful.' Mr Abbott raised his head to watch Laura carefully fixing the electrodes. 'Sure you're not going to give me a shock?' Although he laughed as he asked, Laura recognised the apprehension in his voice, and hastened to reassure him.

'I can assure you it's completely safe and pain-free— the machine just records the potential of the electric currents initiated by your heart muscle. Now, if you could just try to relax and lie still, we'll be finished before you know it.' She switched on the machine, and, while it was still jotting the tracings, indicated to Pam that they could now start removing the electrodes. 'The computer commits the trace to its memory within seconds, so Mr Abbott can move about as much as he likes.'

'You were right, it didn't hurt, and I don't think I've enough hairs on my chest to cause a problem!'

'Good. Now we're going to leave you to undress in the bathroom and slip on the robe provided. Dr Farraday shouldn't keep you waiting long.'

After that the morning passed swiftly, and Laura was just congratulating herself on it running more smoothly than she had expected, when Pam appeared, holding her left hand in the air, her face ashen.

'What on earth is the matter?' Laura was almost afraid to ask.

'I've just taken some blood and stabbed myself with the needle.' Pam's voice quavered as she tried to hide her panic.

Laura was aghast. 'You've done what? I told you I'd do it until you were certificated.'

'You were busy in another room, and Brett——'

'Brett what?' thundered Laura.

'He knew I took it in my previous job and asked me to do it. I didn't like——'

'Forget the explanations. Have you cleansed the injury thoroughly under running water?'

Pam nodded, her eyes wide with fear at the consequences of her act.

'Sit down, then. Does Brett know this has happened?'

Pam shook her head.

'What test were you taking the blood for?'

'Routine haematology and chemistry, including liver function tests.'

'I'll check with the lab that they can test the specimens also for hepatitis, otherwise I'll need to ask the patient for another blood sample. He's still with Brett, is he?'

Pam nodded. 'I was trying to help. I never thought it'd cause so much trouble.'

Laura felt desperately sorry for her; she was young and had not thought out the consequences.

'I'm afraid I'll need a sample from you as well. And you'll have to fill out an accident form. I don't suppose you've been vaccinated against hepatitis, have you?'

Laura's relief at Pam's nod was cut short by Pam's adding, 'I haven't had the third one of the course yet. I was going to ask you about that.'

'Let's hope the first two will have given you immunity, and in all probability there was no infection present. But if there is they'll probably suggest you have the gamma globulin anyway. Come on, I'll take that blood now.'

After collecting the sample, Laura helped Pam to complete the accident form, then sent her with it to the director, settling herself to wait for Brett to finish with the patient.

'What a morning! Thank goodness it's lunch——' Noticing Laura's stern features, Brett stopped mid-sentence. 'Something the matter?'

Laura sprang to her feet, saying, 'Could we go back into your consulting-room a moment, Dr Farraday?'

'Dr Farraday again? I'm still being held responsible for my father's transgressions, then,' Brett teased.

Ignoring his attempt to lighten the situation, Laura closed the door of the consulting-room behind them.

'Dr Farraday, you've put a young girl's life at risk this morning.'

Brett stopped and turned incredulously towards her 'I suppose I shouldn't be surprised at this bizarre accusation, after being blamed for ruining your life on Friday.'

'It's a fact. You put Nurse Rainer's life in danger.'

His expression became thunderous. 'And how exactly do you suggest I managed that?'

'By expecting her to take blood samples.'

'But—why has that——?' Mystified, Brett shook his head. 'You're talking in riddles, Laura. Pam is an experienced phlebotomist; I've seen her often enough at the General.'

'Maybe, but as it's an extended procedure she's not allowed to take blood until she's been re-certificated by our manangement. You obviously pressurised her to do so.'

'And because she didn't have a certificate I've put her life in danger! I've heard everything now!'

'She sustained a needlestick injury——'

'And having a little piece of paper would make that all right? Come off your high horse, Laura, you're talking nonsense. And what about Pam? Is she left unattended while you harangue me?'

'Of course not. I've taken all the prescribed steps and she's with the director now!'

'Great—and your job is to lay the blame at my door? Well, I can——'

'I'm amazed, Dr Farraday, that you treat the matter so lightly.' Laura was determined not to listen to his excuses. 'Not only was she not approved for the task, but she was untrained in the use of the vacuum system. So perhaps you'll be prepared to compensate her for any subsequent ill effects, because under the circumstances the Wellstead will certainly wriggle out of responsibility.'

'Oh, Laura!' Brett seated himself at his desk and covered his face with his hands. After a moment he spoke, but without looking at her. 'Of course I'm worried if this type of accident happens to any member of staff, but I didn't realise the situation, and Pam said nothing when I asked her to take the blood.'

'You mean she didn't tell you I'd told her not to?'

Brett swivelled round in his chair to face her. 'Of course she didn't. What do you take me for? If she'd explained I'd have understood.'

'But. . .' Laura hesitated, trying to recall exactly what Pam had said, 'I thought——'

'You jumped to the conclusion that I'd overruled your orders. Is that it? The other evening, I really began to think we were on the same wavelength. But I was wrong, wasn't I? You still have a pretty low opinion of me.'

It was Laura's turn to adopt a defensive attitude. 'If I'm wrong, I'm sorry. Pam did give me the impression that you insisted, but I can't remember her exactly saying so.'

Brett leapt up and began drumming a tattoo on the floor with his foot.

Realising she had perhaps gone too far, Laura started to apologise. 'I'm sorry, Brett, I didn't——'

But he was past listening to reason. The anger he had been attempting to bottle up spilled out, and with a thunderous expression he exclaimed, 'You never have given me half a chance! Since I returned, everything I've done has been a cause for complaint, and every approach I've made to you has been thrown back in my face. Even what my family did in the past is my fault. Well, at least I know where I stand. I'm not prepared to give up my work here, but there's no need for us to see one another otherwise.' Casting a withering look in her direction, Brett strode from the room and disappeared rapidly along the corridor.

Laura shuddered, knowing without a doubt that she had tried the patience of the amiable Dr Farraday once too often. Recalling how everyone who knew him spoke of his easygoing personality, she kicked herself for provoking such an outburst, realising now that it was too late that she deserved every bit of the criticism levelled at her.

After she had slowly walked the length of the department, it became obvious that Brett must have gone down for lunch, so Laura decided to make do with a cup of coffee in the department.

When Pam returned from her uncomfortable interview with the director, Laura made the excuse that she had too much to do.

'Once you get down the stairs, Pam, you can't miss the dining-room, and you'll find Brett and Marianne in there.'

As she watched Pam along to the stairs, Laura wondered how different the situation might have been if it had not been for Marianne. Laura would have welcomed Brett back from his sabbatical without any of the preconceived reservations Marianne had fed her, and no doubt the same was true for him. Marianne had ensured that their first encounter would be acrimonious by telling Brett that Laura had cancelled his appointment. And, unwittingly, Laura had abetted Marianne's plans. Conscious only of the need to defend her position, she had attacked first, alienating Brett from the start.

She could see only too clearly that whenever she had been with Brett she had acted in a way totally foreign to her usual behaviour, and she tried to work out why. It took the whole of the lunch-hour for her to admit to herself that his initial criticism of her appointment had made her try to live up to Sister Jones's reputation. In attempting to ensure that he could find no fault, she had gone over the top in insisting that everything be done correctly. And the stupid part was that she had repeatedly offended the very person she was trying to impress, and had felt too constrained to respond when he offered her an olive branch.

Recalling the number of times she had refused to believe his interest in her, she was devastated to learn that she had so misread his motives that she had now thrown away any hope of a relationship between them. Lost in thought, Laura was still lingering in the coffee-room, wondering how she could ever make amends, when Dot Griffiths arrived on duty.

'Hi,' Laura greeted her wanly. 'Coffee?'

Dot shook her head. 'No—I'll get the rooms ready for the afternoon.'

'Not just yet, Dot. As it's Staff Nurse Rainer's first day, she's coming back after lunch to learn the routine.'

Laura went on to describe the problems that had arisen that morning, confiding Brett's reaction to her accusations.

Dot frowned. 'I've never known Brett in a temper, although I have heard it happens if you push him too far.'

Laura sighed. 'Oh, dear, I'm going to have to eat humble pie, aren't I?'

Raising her eyebrows in a warning gesture, Dot

smiled ruefully. 'You can try, but it'll be difficult. I gather once you lose his trust it's not easy to regain.'

As Pam returned at that moment, Laura was left again to her own thoughts, knowing that her resentment of her father's continued suffering was inexplicably tied up with her antagonism towards Brett. Although she had found it impossible to accept their different lifestyles, it obviously hadn't worried Brett. But, however much she might regret it, she knew it was too late now. There was no way she would be offered his friendship again, especially after her behaviour that morning.

When he returned with Marianne, he walked past Laura without speaking, and she realised just how badly she must have hurt him for him to behave in such a way. She followed him into his consulting-room.

'I really am sorry, Brett, I know I was unreasonable——'

He did not allow her to finish, but dismissed her apology as unimportant.

'Please forget the matter. I have. I'm ready to start my afternoon list.'

Laura left the room with a heavy heart, knowing that, far from forgetting the matter, he was nursing his resentment.

It was towards the end of the afternoon when Phil Munroe came looking for Brett. 'Is he near the end of his list?'

'He's just finishing, Phil. Have a cup of coffee while you wait.'

'Great. I'm hoping Brett might be free to go up to London tomorrow.' Phil took a sip from the cup Laura proffered.

'London?'

'Mm. You probably heard about the girl needing colposcopy before disappearing to Zambia on a teaching contract?'

'Yes, Peggy Andrews mentioned her.'

'Well, I've contacted the firm and they're delivering some of the bits and pieces tomorrow, but the cold coagulator is in London, and if Brett would like to collect it they're going to give him training in it's use. I'm operating, so I can't manage it, but it would be great if we could sort this girlie out before she goes. Do you know where Brett's working tomorrow?'

'He's here all day today and Thursday morning. Apart from that I don't know.'

Brett's door opened at that moment and he ushered out the managing director of a nearby electronics firm. Returning through the swing doors, he greeted Phil briefly. 'I've been trying to persuade Mr Richards to send more than his senior management for health checks, but I'm not sure I've succeeded—apart from cervical smears. He's more than willing for the female workforce to be given that facility, but only if we could take a mobile unit to the site. I'll have to chat up Mr Edwards again.'

'If he agrees to that it'll be more important than ever to get our new unit under way, and that's what I came to see you about.' Phil emerged from the coffee-room to chat with Brett in the corridor. 'Can you go to London tomorrow?'

'London? Yes, I suppose so, but why?'

Laura felt trapped into listening to the conversation, but since she did not want to push past Phil into Brett's line of vision there was no other way of escape.

Phil went on to explain how the unit could be ready for operation on Wednesday if Brett could collect the treatment machine and learn how to use it. Turning to Laura, he smiled, 'You'll be able to find us a nurse, won't you?'

Brett, noticing her for the first time, looked sceptical.

'No problem. Our new Staff Nurse is working all day this week to learn the ropes, so there'll be three of us on Wednesday afternoon.' Laura was thankful she could give the answer they wanted.

'Would that be convenient for you, Brett? I can manage to be here about three.'

'I should think I could manage that, if Sister is sure it won't spoil the perfect symmetry of her appointment book,' Brett added derisively.

Determined he wouldn't see the scalding heat suffusing her cheeks, Laura turned away as she announced haughtily, 'Three o'clock will be fine by me. Now if you'll excuse me, I must go and help Dot.'

As she hurried down the corridor, she wondered if Brett would tell Phil the reason for his obvious hostility.

She was about to go off duty when Phil came looking for her. Detecting no change in his attitude, she guessed Brett had said nothing, and with a sinking heart knew that his bottling it up meant she had hurt Brett even more deeply than she had imagined.

'Meditec are delivering the couch and colposcope around lunchtime tomorrow,' Phil told her. 'Brett will collect the necessary instruments with the coagulator and bring them in on Wednesday, so can you get some acetic acid and aqueous iodine?'

Having learnt from the book Brett had lent her that

these were the lotions used to demonstrate any abnormality on the cervix, Laura had already put them on order. 'Certainly. Anything else?'

'I don't think so. It's great to have someone so enthusiastic in charge here. While we're on the subject, what was the matter with Brett today? He didn't seem his usual amiable self.'

'I think I upset him this morning. No doubt it'll all blow over.' Laura hastened to reassure Phil, unwilling for him to know just how deep was the rift between them.

'Right, I'll be away, then. I'll pop in tomorrow evening to check what's arrived.'

The Tuesday morning session was well under way when Pam told Laura there was a phone call for her.

'The caller sounds extremely distressed,' she whispered as Laura lifted the receiver. 'I couldn't even get a name.'

'Hello. Can I help you? Sister Pennington speaking.'

'Is that Laura? It's Brett's mother—I met you the other night. Do you know how I can reach Brett? It's urgent.'

'No, but I can try and find out. Is there anything I can do to help in the meantime?'

'It's Mr Farraday—he's in great pain. I want Brett to see him.'

'Can't one of the other doctors at the practice help you?'

'Father refuses to see anyone but Brett—please try and find him for me!'

Laura reassured her, and set about contacting Phil. Phil was incommunicado in the operating theatre, so Laura tried Meditec, who gave her the number of the firm Brett was visiting. But they were unable to help. One of the salesmen had taken him out to lunch not long before and no one knew where they had gone or when they would be back.

'Lunch? At this hour?' Laura checked her watch as she replaced the receiver and saw that it was indeed nearly twelve. There was nothing for it but to ring Mrs Farraday and tell her she'd left a message for Brett to ring home the moment he returned.

'Hello, it's Laura Pennington.' Explaining the situation, Laura was so worried by Mrs Farraday's state that she asked, 'Can I do anything if I come over in my lunch break?'

'Oh, would you? Father liked you—I'm sure he'd let you look at him—but he doesn't like Brett's partners. He's——'

'Where is his pain?' Laura repeated the question a couple of times, then gave up in the face of Mrs Farraday's demented wittering. 'I'll come now; see you in about ten minutes.'

She rang for a taxi, then explained to Pam what she was doing. 'Dot will be on duty with you this afternoon if I'm not back in time for the start, so don't worry.'

She arrived at the grey mansion anxious about what she was likely to find.

Mr Farraday was in a chair by the library fire, leaning hard over to his right as if to lessen some discomfort. Shooing his agitated wife from the room, he showed Laura where the pain was.

'When did it start?'

'It caught me when I got up from breakfast, and it's getting steadily worse. It's here, under the ribs and up into the shoulder. I've had niggles before, but ignored them.'

'Recently?' Her suspicion of a fever was confirmed when Laura placed a cool hand on his forehead.

'Aye, over the last couple of days. Thought I'd probably lifted something awkward on the building site. You know, muscles get a bit lax when you've been on holiday.'

'Have you felt well up to today?'

'Funny you should ask that. I've been feeling under the weather for a week or so now. Nothing I could put my finger on, but just not one hundred per cent.'

Laura thought quickly. The only diagnosis that sprang to mind at his description was a sub-phrenic abscess, but she knew they were so rare that it was most unlikely to be that. Attempting to disprove her suspicions, she continued her questioning. When his answers suggested no other condition, she asked in desperation, 'Have you been in hospital for an operation recently?'

Her patient shook his head. 'No, I'm never ill. Can't imagine what's gone wrong this time.'

Laura thought quickly. Sub-phrenic abscesses usually only occurred following surgery. Yet all Mr Farraday's symptoms seemed to point to one. Trying to recall what she had read about them the last time she had nursed one, Laura had a hazy idea that very occasionally one did occur at a primary site. If she was right, delay was dangerous, so she would have to risk the possibility that she might be wrong.

'I think you ought to go to hospital, Mr Farraday, and I don't think you should wait until Brett gets home.'

'Why? What's up with me?'

'I think you might have an infection there, and it's collecting together like a boil, causing the pain. We'll get you to the Westleigh Casualty and see what they say.'

'Nay, you won't, I've paid into private insurance long enough. I want to go to the Wellstead.'

His request put Laura in a difficult position. She could hardly ring a consultant and ask him to admit Brett's father on her diagnosis, and yet she must initiate some action. She wished she knew which of the general surgeons might know Brett.

Eventually she made up her mind to ring Phil Munroe and ask his advice. With luck he would be out of theatre, but would still be at the hospital.

The moment she explained the position to him, Phil understood her predicament. 'Can you get him here and I'll get Brian Hastings to meet you in Outpatients?'

Relieved, Laura explained to Brett's parents that she was calling a taxi to take them all to the Wellstead and that in all probability he would be kept in. Although Mrs Farraday appeared to be pottering ineffectually, she came down the stairs with a large holdall when the taxi arrived. Laura wondered what on earth was in it, but thought it wisest to say nothing. Within minutes of their arriving at the hospital, Brian Hastings examined the patient, prescribed pain relief and arranged a bed for Mr Farraday. Relieved of the responsibility, Laura returned to her department and, discovering all was under control, helped herself to a welcome cup of coffee.

She was only halfway through it when the telephone rang to inform her that the colposcopy equipment was on its way. Laura supervised the delivery and returned to the now tepid liquid, only to be summoned to the telephone again.

'Is that you, Laura? Brett here. I got your message, but no one is answering at home. What's happening, for goodness' sake?'

Laura took a deep breath and launched into a brief explanation of events. When he remained silent she surmised that he was annoyed by the way she had gone about things, so she added curtly, 'I'll put you through to the ward, Brett. Brian is probably still there.' And, without allowing him a chance to reply, she depressed the recall button and rang the ward number.

Before going off duty that evening, Laura contacted the ward sister, and was delighted to learn that her diagnosis had been correct. Mr Hastings was draining the abscess under antibiotic cover and Mr Farraday was already more comfortable. At least Brett could not fault her on the speed of her actions.

Throughout the long evening at home, she half hoped Brett might feel sufficiently grateful to contact her, but it was a forlorn hope. The telephone did not ring once, and at eleven Laura retired to bed disappointed. It was not that she wanted his gratitude, but she had hoped that the actions that had been forced upon her might return their understanding to what it had been the previous week.

However, the knowledge that, if the colposcopy went ahead, she would see him that afternoon lent a lightness to Laura's step as she set out for the Wellstead on Wednesday morning. She couldn't believe Brett would be churlish enough to ignore the help she had given his father, even though he might not be able to completely forgive her outburst. Optimistic that their working relationship could at least return to a semblance of normality, she looked forward to the afternoon session.

However, when Brett came in unexpectedly around mid-morning, his only concern was to check the colposcopy equipment. Laura accompanied him to room five, and breathed a sigh of relief when it appeared that everything met with his approval.

Closing the door behind him, he set off at speed along the corridor. 'I'll be back around two to assist Phil.' His voice was forbidding as he paused at her desk.

'Would you like a cup of coffee?'

'No, thanks. I must dash.' And, before she could ask how his father was, he sped away from the department.

Remembering Dot's comments on Monday afternoon, Laura realised that her actions of the day before had made not the slightest impression on the hurt she had inflicted. Not that that had been her reason for helping the Farradays—she would have done the same for anyone in such distress—but all the same it would have been nice to know that Brett appreciated her actions.

CHAPTER SEVEN

LAURA made sure she was back from lunch in good time to help with the colposcopy. Arriving at her desk, she found an envelope containing the results of Pam's blood test, and saw with relief that Pam was immune to hepatitis. Her relief was intensified by an attached note saying that no infection had been found in the patient's blood. She gave the good news to Pam immediately and put the forms aside to show to Brett.

Leaving Dot and Pam to cope with the screening, she ushered a very worried patient down the corridor.

'Colposcopy's nothing to worry about, Sarah. It's just like having a smear taken, but this time we use a microscope with a light to assist us.' When Sarah appeared interested, Laura continued, 'The scope's telescopic lenses help the doctor to pinpoint any abnormal areas after the cervix has been painted with first weak vinegar, then iodine.'

'Some concoction!' Sarah laughed nervously.

'Kind of a marinade, perhaps?' Laura joked in an attempt to relieve Sarah's nervousness.

Phil and Brett arrived together, and Laura left them to chat with Sarah, not expecting them to be too long as Brett would have taken a gynaecological history from her when she attended for the smear.

When they eventually emerged from the room, Laura was hovering in the corridor.

'Can you get her into position, Sister? I want a brief

word with Brett before we start.' Phil was already concentrating on his conversation with Brett, so Laura moved quietly back into the room.

'I'm as new to this couch as you are, Sarah; it was only delivered yesterday. Now slide your bottom right down to the edge and rest your feet in these. Not an elegant position, I know, but it's soon over.' Covering her with a modesty blanket, Laura chatted about Zambia and teaching to try and take Sarah's mind off the procedure.

The men returned and Phil took the seat behind the colposcope. 'Right, Sarah. Same procedure as for a smear so that I can get a good view.' Phil leaned over to switch on the colposcope as Laura poured out the required solutions and turned her attention to Sarah.

'I'm just taking another smear, Sarah, this time with a brush. Then I'm going to paint your cervix with acetic acid.' Phil handed the brush over to Brett, who transferred the cells to a glass slide and applied a fixative. 'Mm, that's fine. Now I'll use some iodine.'

'Sounds like a Picasso painting,' joked Sarah.

'Ye-es. I can't say I've found anything to get het up about here. All I can see is a tiny abnormal spot. I'm just taking a minute biopsy. Might feel a bit odd, but it shouldn't hurt.'

Laura opened the specimen container as Phil continued, 'Normally I'd leave it alone and repeat this examination in six months, when the problem would more than likely have righted itself. However, as you're disappearing off to Zambia, we'll treat it and then you needn't worry until you return to this country.'

Phil vacated his chair for Brett, who switched on the

cold coagulator and waited for the green light to indicate that it had reached the correct temperature.

'Is that a laser machine?' Sarah was trying to catch a sight of the probes.

'No, there are several different methods of dealing with this problem, and cold coagulation is now thought to be the best. Let me know when twenty seconds is up, Laura.'

His request startled her, especially as it was the first time he had spoken directly to her. However, she quickly checked the watch pinned to her uniform.

'Time's up.'

Brett re-examined the area and, after a further twenty seconds' treatment, removed the instruments. 'All over.'

As Phil and Brett disappeared through the door, Sarah jumped down from the couch, her face wreathed in smiles. 'Gosh, that was nowhere near as bad as I expected.'

'No, it's just the thought that's so awful. The actual procedure is nothing.' Laura was just relieved that everything had gone smoothly at their first attempt.

'Thanks for helping me through it, though.' Sarah was much happier now.

Laura smiled and vacated the room to allow Phil and Brett back to talk with Sarah. When the consultation was finished, Phil had to dash back to the hospital, but Brett called Laura into the room, and she was relieved to discover that his mood was different from his earlier visit.

'Thank you for your help, Laura. I'll show you how to clean these probes. They're made of a kind of non-stick plastic and just need wiping after dipping in normal saline.' Brett opened a sachet of the liquid as he spoke.

'What about sterilising them?'

'That's done by the machine. Press this button and when the orange light goes out they're ready. You can do the same before treatment as well.'

Laura nodded, hardly daring to breathe in case she should again disturb the fragile rapport between them.

When Brett sat down at the desk to complete the pathology form, she moved quietly about the room tidying the trolley and the couch. As she took the form from his hand, Brett caught hold of her other one, saying, 'I'm very grateful for what you did for Dad yesterday.'

Feeling a warmth spreading through her, Laura was about to reply when she noticed he had reached into his pocket and withdrawn a twenty-pound note.

'This should amply cover your expense——'

'I don't want your money!' Laura was so shocked at his intention to reward her financially that she pulled right away from him and stood by the door, glaring.

'Laura, I didn't mean to insult you. I thought——' Brett's voice trailed off as he realised he had indeed done exactly that. 'Oh, for goodness' sake, you've always made it plain how important money is to you——' At Laura's outraged gasp, he stopped again, obviously sensing that he was putting what he believed to be the truth very badly.

Though Laura watched with compunction as the realisation that he was making matters worse slid slowly across his face, she felt unable to meet him even halfway, much as she wanted to. Seeing his behaviour as the final insult in a situation that had already deteriorated to unplumbed depths, she felt the less said the better.

Recognising the impasse, Brett rose to his feet and, momentarily resting a hand on her shoulder, murmured helplessly, 'I'm truly sorry,' and was gone.

Laura remained motionless for several minutes after he left her alone. She wanted so much to believe that she hadn't destroyed all his respect for her, and yet it appeared that even normal conversation was beyond them.

She worked mechanically for the remainder of the week. When Brett arrived for his Thursday morning session, he replied curtly to her enquiry about his father, 'He's going on fine, thanks.'

It was left to Ruth Grimes, the ward sister, to fill her in with all the details over lunch on Friday.

'Everyone seems amazed that you guessed what was wrong with Brett's father. Brett must be more than grateful.'

'Hm. If he is, he doesn't show it.'

Ruth frowned, unable to believe the engaging Dr Farraday capable of such an omission. 'He's been spending a lot of time up on the ward—perhaps he hasn't had a chance to pop down and see you.'

'Perhaps,' Laura agreed, not wanting to discuss it further. 'Has Brian found the cause of the abscess?' She hoped her query would encourage Ruth off the subject of Brett.

'Not really. Apparently when they occur like this they suspect that a sub-clinical peritonitis must have occurred in the previous weeks. I suppose Mr Farraday is such a fit man that he fought off the original infection, and it's only just caught up with him. Brian has ordered a myriad investigations to try and discover the cause.' Ruth clattered her cutlery on to her plate and went in search of a sweet course. 'I think he'll probably be discharged early next week and have most of them done as an outpatient, more's the pity. Brett Farraday doesn't come up to the ward normally.'

Irritated by Ruth's hero-worship, Laura checked the time, and reluctantly decided to return to the department.

Phil was waiting for her. 'Can we book a colposcopy list on a regular basis, Laura? Preferably on Wednesday afternoon. I've already had a couple of enquiries.'

'I don't see why not. It's about our lightest day, so it would be ideal.'

'I shan't be able to come on a regular basis, but Brett will take the list in my absence.'

Laura nodded, making her mind up there and then that on Brett's days Dot could assist with the list. The last thing she wanted was for patients to sense an atmosphere between them, and she was afraid that was more than likely if they worked in the close proximity of the colposcopy room.

During the weekend, which Laura spent assisting her father in any way she could, she detected a deterioration in his ability to move around, no doubt due to an increase in the pain. Reflecting on the speed with which Mr Farraday had had attention, she felt all her misgivings about her position at the Wellstead return.

'I'm going to ring Dad's consultant tomorrow,' she told her mother after they had helped him to bed on the Sunday evening. 'Dad's definitely getting worse, and he must surely be near the top of the list by now.'

'Do you think it'll do any good?'

'Difficult to say, but it's worth a try. Might just nudge them into taking him sooner rather than later.'

However, the next day all thought of her father was driven from her mind. One of the Sunday tabloids had run an article saying that, despite the low uptake of cervical smears, it was estimated that over a third of the results were inaccurate, leaving a large percentage of the female population at risk from cervical cancer. The rest of the media had blown the story up out of all proportion.

As always happened with these scare stories, lines to the Wellstead were jammed by worried females requesting an early appointment for a smear.

Marianne's extension was permanently engaged, so the switchboard re-routed calls to Laura.

However, Laura soon discovered that Peggy Andrews's sessions were fully booked for several weeks ahead.

'Don't make any more appointments, Marianne. Take the telephone numbers and we'll try to organise extra sessions. It's the only way we're going to cope with this deluge.'

As soon as Peggy finished with her first well woman screen, Laura confronted her with the appointment book.

'Can you possibly fit in at least one extra session a week, if not two?'

Peggy shook her head. 'I'm sorry, Laura, I don't have a moment spare as it is. The practice is getting so much busier that I may have to give up this session soon.'

'Do you know anybody who might be willing to take it on? Preferably female.'

Again Peggy's reply was negative. 'I'll ask around, but it might be difficult finding a suitably qualified replacement. What about Brett? He coped with my list that day I was ill, and he was saying only the other day how much free time he has.'

Laura sighed. 'I suppose it might be the answer.'

'But not ideal, eh?' teased Peggy. 'I'm very convenient, not requiring a chaperon, aren't I?'

Laura nodded her agreement, not daring to admit that the staffing levels had never entered her mind. She was more concerned that it would mean Brett's visits to the department increasing, and she wasn't at all sure she could cope with that.

However, by the time he took a break for coffee, the backlog on requests for appointments was so great that Laura swallowed her pride and acquainted him with the problem.

'I'm not surprised. When I heard the news last night I expected something like this, but not here. I thought it would be the neighbourhood doctors who'd be inundated.'

'Apparently one programme last night said you were more likely to get an accurate result from the private sector. Goodness knows what gave them that idea, but I think it's quite a dangerous concept. It's pushing people to find money for smears unnecessarily.'

'Your social conscience is working overtime, Laura. I can't see the price of a smear reducing anybody to the breadline.'

'Hm. But if we get flooded with requests, there's a danger we'll be too rushed to do the job properly. I'm already pushed into looking for a doctor to do extra sessions.'

'And you might have to accept someone you don't consider suitable.' Brett's face broke into the lop-sided grin Laura had not been favoured with for some time. 'That's my Laura! Thanks for the vote of confidence.'

Anxiety clouding her judgement, Laura did not recognise that he was joking, and retorted. 'You're deliberately misunderstanding me. You know perfectly well I'd rather turn people away than give a second-class service.'

Brett shook his head dolefuly. 'I do tend to put things badly. I wouldn't dare imply that the Wellstead's standards could suffer. However, I think you should bear in mind the extra workload for the pathology staff. Perhaps you ought to check their moral stance. You might even find they're only doing it for the money.'

This time recognising the mocking tone of his voice, Laura snapped, 'I wouldn't expect you to appreciate the responsibility I have as head of this department.'

Brett raised a questioning eyebrow at the vehemence of her reply. 'Oh, yes, I would.' He rose from his seat and assuming a threatening stance, towered menacingly over her. 'That message comes over loud and clear.'

Laura felt hot colour scorching her cheeks as she realised how her efforts to run the department efficiently had been misinterpreted.

'I don't think you understood——'

However, Brett ignored her blustering as with consummate indifference he enquired, 'When could you fit in some extra sessions? As you probably know, I've quite a lot of free time still.'

Relieved that the awkward moment was past, Laura enumerated, 'Tomorrow. Possibly Thursday afternoon if we use the colposcopy room, and, I suppose, all day Friday.'

Brett consulted his diary. 'I could manage Tuesday afternoon, in fact I'm free all day Tuesday, but only Friday afternoon.' He raised his eyes to see how Laura would take his next statement. 'Until we get the backlog cleared, I could do evening sessions.'

She hesitated. She didn't want to refuse him outright, but, although she wouldn't object to working overtime for a while, there was always the problem of her father at the back of her mind. It was a struggle for her mother to get him to bed on her own, and he seemed to want to go earlier and earlier these days.

'Er—I suppose we could manage, provided they don't run on too late.'

Brett did not answer immediately. 'Surely you wouldn't have to cover them all? What about Pam and Dot?'

'They both took part-time jobs so they could look after their families. I can ask them, but I can't insist. It wouldn't be fair.'

'And you like your evenings free too.' Brett's tone was sententious, making Laura wonder if he thought she used her father as an excuse to allow her freedom to enjoy herself.

Recalling his giving Marianne the benefit of the doubt, she bristled with suppressed fury at his intolerance where she was concerned. 'I do, yes. As my father gets increasingly incapacitated, I like to help my mother. She has enough to cope with during the day.'

Brett was immediately contrite. 'I didn't realise things were so bad. Perhaps he could be re-designated as an urgent case now?'

'I did wonder. I was going to ring Mr Hawkins's secretary today, but this onslaught hasn't given me a chance.' Laura didn't confess her reluctance to telephone in case she was seen as trying to jump the queue.

Brett checked his watch. 'I mustn't keep the next chap waiting. Perhaps we could sort some sessions out over lunch.'

Laura nodded her agreement, and returned to her task of answering the many queries that were still being put through to her.

As lunchtime approached, she told the switchboard to hold all telephone calls and made for Marianne's office.

'I've asked the switchboard to suggest people ring back after two, so you should get a respite now. I think Brett is going to do some extra sessions, so perhaps you'd take the diary down to lunch and we can arrange when they'll be.'

Marianne appeared delighed to do so, and Laura guessed it could only be due to the promised increase in work for her favourite doctor.

'Can I use some evenings, then, Laura?' Brett was checking his diary. They were seated round a small dining-table, and Laura noticed that Marianne was anxiously awaiting her answer.

'A couple to start with, but to finish no later than eight. OK?'

The relief that flashed across Marianne's face as she spoke left Laura busily wondering what Brett thought of such obvious hero-worship.

Brett broke in on her reverie. 'How about a Tuesday afternoon session running on into the evening, and, until we get the colposcopy really under way, an evening session on Wednesday?'

'Sounds all right.'

'And you'll ask Dot and Pam if they can help out some evenings?' Brett had obviously not forgotten their earlier conversation, and Laura was touched by his thoughtfulness when she had shown so little trust in him.

She nodded, although she had no intention of shirking her duties. She felt it was her place to cover the clinics, and, if it meant her doing extra hours, too bad. Her father would just have to go to bed a little later than usual.

They all returned to the department early, and Marianne set about ringing back some of the morning's callers, to arrange for appointments the next day.

Laura saw little of Brett for the remainder of the afternoon, and when she was ready to go off duty he and Marianne were poring over the diary, so rather than disturb them she left unobtrusively, only remembering on her way out that she had still done nothing about an early appointment for her father.

Tuesday was nearly as busy with enquiries as Monday had been, and, coming out of consulting-room four at coffee-time, Laura was surprised to see Brett in the corridor. However, watching him into the office, she presumed he was in early to lunch with Marianne.

As she had thought, when she and Pam went down to the dining-room, Marianne and Brett were already there, deep in conversation. The moment Laura joined them, their chat stopped, and Laura sensed an embarrassed silence descending.

Brett eyed Laura's salad critically. 'If you're working

until eight you need something more substantial than that.'

Laura smiled and shook her head. 'Mum will have prepared a cooked meal for this evening, and one a day is plenty, otherwise my uniform won't fasten.'

Brett's eyes swept over the parts of her uniform he could see and shook his head. 'I can't believe that, but I'll no doubt be in trouble if I try to discourage healthy eating in this place!'

Laura assigned Dot to look after Dr Thoms for the afternoon, leaving herself to prepare and chaperon Brett's patients. As the afternoon wore on into the evening, she sensed the initial tension between them gradually evaporate.

When the session was at last over, Laura felt Brett's eyes on her as she quickly tidied the room and washed the few remaining instruments.

As she emerged from the bathroom, he leaned back in his swivel chair and indicated the armchair by the desk. 'Take the weight off your feet for a few moments. I want to talk to you.'

Apprehensively, Laura did as he asked.

'First of all, I'm not asking, but I'm telling you. I'm running you home from these late sessions.' Laura smiled her acquiescence. She was so tired she would have agreed to drive home with Dracula. In fact, she experienced a perverse pleasure at the thought of being alone with him throughout the journey.

'Secondly,' Brett leaned back again and placed the tips of his fingers together, 'I came in this morning to see Mr Hawkins's secretary in the hopes of having a word with him. However, he's away at a conference all week. I asked about an appointment next week, but his list is overflowing. In fact, it appears Mr Hawkins won't be able to see your father until next month. But,' he held up a hand to prevent her intended interruption, 'she suggested I had a word with him myself, letting him know how much your dad's condition has deteriorated since he last saw him. Apparently he's so overworked that he'll take my word for it.'

Overwhelmed by his actions, Laura had difficulty in holding back her tears. It had been a long day and her weariness made it difficult to keep her emotions in check, especially when she recalled the strained atmosphere of the past week.

'That's great, Brett.' Overcoming the urge to cry, she lifted her head to discover his keen gaze waiting diffidently to see how she would react to his interference. Hastening to reassure him before she lost another opportunity to make amends, she realised just how perceptive he had been. He had sensed her reluctance to contact the surgeon, and, far from being the playboy she had first thought, he repeatedly demonstrated a caring side of his character that she hadn't believed existed.

She attempted to reward him with an encouraging smile, but at the same time lost the battle with her tears. She felt them trickling down her cheeks as she murmured, 'Oh, Brett, it really is kind of you to go to so much trouble—I do appreciate it.'

Relieved, Brett quietly proffered the box of tissues, first removing one to dab tenderly at her eyes. When the flow of tears began to dry up, he gently took both her hands in his. 'The last thing I intended was to upset you. I want to help.' When Laura did not answer he continued, 'Your work is taxing enough without the further responsibility of your father. Instead of coming back fresh from your weekend off, you looked exhausted yesterday.'

Laura's shrug was deprecatory. 'I don't mind, and you know there are hundreds of people in the same position.'

'Maybe, but I only care about you.'

His totally unexpected words sent a high-powered exhilaration pulsing through her veins, until rational thought reminded her that he only wanted to make sure she was fit for duty. The disappointment caused her to recover abruptly from her romancing, and she attempted to pull her hands free.

Brett rose to his feet, pulling her up with him. He shook his head. 'Poor little Laura, so used to caring for others that you shun anyone who tries to do the same for you. Come on, let's get out of here.'

Still holding one hand, Laura allowed herself to be led from the department.

'I need to get my coat from the changing-room.' They had reached the front waiting area, so Brett took a seat and picked up the nearest magazine. 'I'll wait.'

As Laura scurried down the stairs and changed out of her uniform, her mind was a tumult of emotion. If only Brett realised just how much she wanted him to care, but not in the way he meant. Although she would never have believed it possible, she had stupidly allowed him to worm his way insidiously into her heart. Sensing the present arousal of her feelings, Laura wondered if she was even sensible in accepting his offer of a lift home. Deciding she could do nothing else, she returned to meet him at the front entrance, pausing only to switch off the lights in her department on the way.

He rose to greet her with a smile that sent her heart lurching painfully. As they made for the car park, Brett draped an arm lightly around her shoulder, and she shuddered, knowing her instincts downstairs had been right. She was playing with fire, and it was already beginning to burn.

CHAPTER EIGHT

THEY walked silently to the car, Laura knowing she must be careful to say nothing to offend Brett after his efforts on her father's behalf.

As he climbed into the driver's seat, a sudden thought struck her. 'You said Mr Hawkins would accept your word about the deterioration in Dad's condition, but there's no way you can know, is there?'

Starting the engine, Brett turned a surprised look on her. 'I accept what you tell me. I do trust *you*, you know.'

Laura chewed her lip thoughtfully as they drove out of the hospital grounds. Maybe he did trust her, but he still hadn't completely forgiven her lack of trust in him. She felt her cheeks colouring at the thought, and wished desperately that they had not got off to such a bad start. However much improved their understanding was, there seemed no way she could make amends for her hurtful behaviour. It was a regret she would have to live with for the rest of her life, for she would never know what might have been if she hadn't been so hostile towards him.

'Penny for them?' Brett removed his left hand from the steering-wheel and placed it over hers.

'Oh—er—I was thinking about Dad. And the future.'

'And what do you think the future might hold for you?'

122

Laura sighed. 'If Dad has his operation, perhaps easier times?'

'That wasn't exactly what I meant, and you know it.' Brett increased the pressure on her hand. 'How about relaxing over a drink before tackling your insurmountable problems?'

Laura tried to think rationally about his suggestion as the emotions raised by just the touch of his hand urged her to agree. 'I'm sorry, Brett.' And this time she really meant it. 'I must go straight home.'

However, he must have sensed her reluctance, for, instead of swinging round into her road, he drove a little way past and pulled into the kerb where the road widened.

Turning slowly, he drew her gently into his arms, until their faces were no more than an inch apart. After regarding her solemnly for what seemed like an eternity, he bent to gently caress her lips with his own. When she made no move of protest, he increased the pressure, demanding and taking possession of the honeyed penetralia beyond. Aroused as her tongue explored the masculine taste of his lips, Laura felt the tips of her breasts tingle and grow taut in anticipation.

As he pulled her even closer, she felt his heart echoing the pounding beat of her own. Oblivious to the passage of time, she abandoned all thoughts of her urgency to get home.

It was only when he attempted to nudge her jumper aside that Laura called a halt. 'I—I'm sorry, Brett, I really must get home.'

The anguish that filled his eyes as she pulled away was reflected by the utter desolation she herself experienced the moment they were apart.

Yet, in that moment, Laura recognised the danger of yielding to her desires—not only because she was so unsure of him, but also because her parents would be anxiously awaiting her arrival home.

Straightening her clothes, she murmured, 'I can walk from here. Thanks for the lift, Brett.'

As she hastily checked her appearance in the driving mirror, he placed a restraining hand on her lap.

'No way. I intend to take you right home. And perhaps meet your father?' he queried tentatively.

'What? Oh, yes.' Recalling Brett's attempts to help, Laura felt a surge of guilt wash over her. She should have realised he would rather speak to Mr Hawkins from personal experience. 'You're more than welcome,' she added lamely.

Despite knowing she had no option, she felt apprehensive as he parked his car just inside the drive. Their council house would surely seem like a rabbit hutch to him after life in his parents' mansion.

Opening the front door to be greeted by her mother, Laura made a hasty introduction. 'Mum, this is Brett Farraday. He gave me a lift home, as we finished late.'

Her mother welcomed him warmly and led the way into the front room to meet her husband. Laura followed silently, and was surprised to see how at home Brett immediately appeared as he took the seat opposite her father.

After a brief chat, Brett asked if he could assist in any way. 'I've a pair of good strong arms.'

Wanting to shout, I know that only too well! Laura merely described the way they usually got her father upstairs, and Brett assured them he could manage on his own.

'Can I get you a drink, then, or a cup of coffee?' Laura was eager to make amends for her earlier omission.

'Just coffee, please, I'm on call tonight.' Then as an afterthought, 'What about your meal? It's not spoiling, is it?'

'It'll reheat in the microwave when she's ready.' Mrs Pennington smiled approvingly at his consideration. 'But can we get you anything? You must be just as hungry.'

'No, thanks, I've a meal waiting as well.'

Laura wondered briefly who had the meal ready for him, then, guessing it was his mother, smiled as she heard the two men chatting on their way up the stairs, and as Brett got her father to bed, the smile changed to one of contentment. Their not getting on was something she didn't need to worry about.

When Brett came down, Mrs Farraday joined her husband upstairs with their evening drinks.

Brett sipped his coffee. 'Thanks for this, Laura.'

'Thanks for what you've just done. It usually takes Mum and me twice as long.'

Brett smiled. 'No problem. I was glad to do it.' After a moment's pause when Laura felt his eyes were devouring her, he frowned. 'Your father is a lot worse than I was expecting. It's scandalous to think that he could be relieved of all that pain. I wonder you haven't tried to pull a few strings before this.'

Laura shrugged. 'It's not all that easy. It might be for the medical professsion, but not for nurses, that's why I was so grateful for the trouble you took to see Mr Hawkins's secretary. I was dreading the usual rebuff.'

Brett shook his head in disgust. 'I'll do the best I can next week.'

'You didn't say anything to Dad, did you?' Laura asked anxiously. 'I don't want to raise his hopes unnecessarily.'

'No, I wouldn't do that. We did have quite a chat, though. Sounds as if working in the Patent Office was a fascinating job.

Laura agreed. 'Yes, full of interest, which he always said compensated for the poor level of pay. He was sorry when ill-health forced him to give it up.'

Her mother joined them then, and not long afterwards Brett took his leave, but not before he had reassured them both. 'We're working late again tomorrow, so I'll see Laura home safely and help Mr Pennington to bed again.'

As Laura saw him to his car, she felt strangely ill at ease. 'Thanks again, Brett.'

'Thank you. See you tomorrow.' Brett took both her hands in his and, pulling her towards him, dropped a kiss lightly on her lips, but before she had recovered he was gone, making Laura wonder again where he was rushing off to.

'He seems very pleasant,' her mother greeted her on her return.

Laura agreed, but her emotions were too mixed up to want to discuss him further, and she asked if there was anything else she could do. 'If not, I'm off to bed. I'm too tired even to think.'

Her mother looked surprised but made no comment. 'No, there's nothing. Goodnight, love.'

Despite the tiredness she had pleaded, Laura found her mind uncooperative. Thoughts of Brett chased

to chaperon, she was ready to perform the tasks he requested with a minimum of fuss.

The moment he finished with Mrs Talbot, she handed him the notes of the next patient for a smear. She continued that way throughout the evening, until he begged for mercy.

'Aren't I entitled to a cup of coffee? I was up with Dad for a couple of hours before I started, and I'm parched!'

'He's still an in-patient, then? How is he?' Laura asked as she poured the coffee. Anything to keep on neutral subjects.

'He's great in himself; the abscess appears to have resolved satisfactorily. He's still having a few tests, but Brian Hastings believes his problem was caused by widespread diverticulosis. He thinks one of the diverticula must have become infected and leaked its contents into the abdomen—hence the abscess.' Brett drained his coffee cup and picked up the next set of notes.

'Would it have resealed itself?' Laura couldn't believe such a thing possible.

'Apparently it can happen if the patient is very fit. His own immune system would do that, but it obviously couldn't cope with the residual infection. If it had, we'd never have known anything about it. Anyway, I must get on.'

Laura knew Marianne was still in the office, no doubt catching up on the work she had missed during yet another morning off. Knowing the secretary would sense her disapproval, she kept well away.

She was just thinking that as the last patient was in

with Brett she could start to tidy the other rooms, when he came looking for her.

'Laura, do you think we could colposcope this lassie now?'

'Now? Why?'

'She's already had an abnormal smear result from the family planning clinic and panicked. She tried to ignore it until this hoo-ha in the media, and now she's so frightened, she hoped we'd disagree with the earlier result. I don't think she'll have the courage to return if we send her away.'

'B—but. . .' Laura stammered, unsure of how to go on, 'would Mr Munroe approve?'

'What do you mean?'

'You told me yourself he was training you in the speciality. I just wondered if you should undertake this without supervision.'

'Your trust in me is touching! For goodness' sake, if I can take a smear I can do this. It's in the interpretation of results that I need help, and I've no intention of doing that alone. Have a bit of faith in me, will you?'

Laura felt the colour flooding her cheeks. 'OK, OK, I'll set it up.'

'Thanks.' Brett looked anything but grateful. 'When you're ready I'll bring her along.'

As the equipment was all prepared in room five, Laura checked it briefly and went to collect the patient.

'Give me a shout when you're ready.' Brett was busy writing in her notes.

As soon as the patient saw the colposcope she clutched Laura's arm. 'Is this going to hurt? He said it wouldn't, but I. . .'

'No, I can assure you it won't hurt. Look, this is just a microscope with a light through which the doctor can see what's happening. As far as you're concerned, it's just like having an ordinary smear. Just slip the clothes from your lower half and hop up on to this couch, and it'll be over before you know it.'

'Will the cancer have spread because I ignored it?'

Laura didn't think she'd ever seen a patient quite so anxious before—perhaps this was the reason why. She obviously didn't understand her smear result and thought she already had cancer.

'An abnormal smear doesn't mean you've got cancer. It just detects a pre-cancerous state on your cervix. Now just relax back on the pillow. Dr Farraday won't be long.'

'What causes the abnormality?' The girl was clearly still not convinced.

'Nobody really knows. There are various theories in circulation——'

'It's a virus transmitted sexually, isn't it?'

Laura took her hand in an attempt to reassure her. 'That idea comes from the fact that abnormal smears appear more often in people who've suffered from genital warts, but, as I said before, there's absolutely no proof. It's just a suggestion.'

Brett had entered the room as Laura spoke, and, assessing the situation, he added, 'We can't be certain, but many gynaecologists think that if the abnormality is left alone it will right itself. But, and it's a big but, if we don't treat it it's essential to have repeat smears very regularly to check that there's been no spread.'

The patient gave Laura a wan smile. 'Oh, dear, I do worry so!'

Laura hastened to reassure her. 'You're not alone. We all worry when it's our own health at stake.'

'Let's get on, shall we?' Brett warmed the speculum. 'Now, if you can relax, this won't hurt at all.'

Laura was as relieved as the patient when Brett announced that the abnormality was a minute patch which he could either treat or leave a while to see if it reverted to normal without help. 'I've taken another smear, and now I'll take a biopsy and make the decision when we have the result from the laboratory. There, all finished now. You can hop down and get dressed.' His tone was sharper than usual, and Laura knew it was probably her fault.

Brett left the room leaving Laura to help the girl down and continue her reassurance. By the time they returned to Brett, the patient appeared much happier.

'Thanks, Laura.' Brett gave her a winsome smile as she left the room, but Laura ignored it and went to clear up the colposcopy equipment. When she had finished, she checked room four, but Brett had disappeared. She crossed to the office, intending to ask him if he had finished. What she saw made her clutch at her stomach.

Marianne was sitting in the one comfortable chair in the office and Brett was kneeling in front of her. He was wiping away tears from her eyes the way he had done for Laura the night before.

But it was what he was saying that caused Laura the most pain. 'You wait here. I've promised to take Laura home and I can't let her down, but I'll come back for you as soon as I can.'

Laura didn't wait for Marianne's reply. Muttering, 'Not on your life, I can get myself home,' she strode to her desk and telephoned for a taxi. Slipping downstairs,

she changed quickly out of her uniform, then returned
to the department to find Marianne and Brett still
ensconced in the office. When Reception rang through
to say her taxi was waiting, Laura strode down the
corridor, called into the office, 'I'm off now,' and made
for the exit.

'Laura!' Brett's call was reproachful as he followed
her down the corridor. 'Laura, where are you going?'

'Home. I've a taxi waiting.' Before Brett could catch
up with her, she slipped through the swing doors.

As they swung to, she heard Brett's voice faintly.
'But Laura, I was going to take you home!'

Giving the driver her address, she sat back and
closed her eyes, relieved to be away from any confron-
tation. That could wait until the morning, when Brett
would no doubt demand an explanation. She didn't
expect he would try to contact her at home, and she
wasn't disappointed, confirming her suspicions that he
saw her as nothing more than a charity case.

As they helped her father to bed, she fobbed off all
her mother's questions by saying that Brett had been
called out.

She was not looking forward to his arrival for the
Thursday morning list, but she had certainly not antici-
pated the extent of his fury. In fact she had expected
no more than a token protest, for hadn't she made it
possible for him to take Marianne home without delay?

As it was, he arrived early, striding into the consulting-room she was setting out and grasping her roughly
by the upper arms, almost shaking her with his rage.

'And just what were you playing at last night?'

Intimidated, Laura remained silent.

'You knew I'd arranged to take you home and help

your father. Your parents must have a pretty poor opinion of me for letting them down!'

'No, they haven't. I told them you were called out.'

Brett stared at her with astonishment. 'That's not the point, is it? Would you mind telling me what you're playing at?'

'I just thought Marianne's need was greater than mine. I could make my own way home.'

Exasperated, Brett threw her back against the consulting-room couch. 'I don't believe it!'

Covering his face with his hands, he strode from the room, obviously too overcome by emotion to harangue her further.

Shaken, Laura continued her tasks, trying to put all thoughts of Brett from her conscious mind. She wasn't helped by Marianne arriving an hour late and being at her most difficult.

'It's past nine, Marianne; where are this morning's lists?'

'I haven't had time to start them. Here are the notes—you'll have to make your own.'

'Why didn't you do them yesterday?'

'I got right behind with all those phone calls earlier in the week, and they're still coming.'

'But you did some overtime last night?'

'Hm. Didn't get much done, then, did I?'

'I don't know, Marianne, but I don't see why not. There was no one to disturb you.'

'Maybe not.' Marianne put an end to the conversation by donning her audio earphones and recommencing her typing.

Irritated, Laura took the notes along to her desk and wrote out a list.

The day progressed in a similar pattern. If anything could go wrong, it did. Brett's first appointment arrived late, then overran her allotted time. Laura and Pam spent the morning soothing ruffled customers who were kept waiting.

When Laura offered the second lady a cup of coffee, she discovered the fuse had blown in the coffee machine and she was pouring tepid liquid into the cup. When she rang the engineer he was off the site, supposedly obtaining spare parts.

As the morning clinic overran the lunch-hour, Laura decided to give food a miss, but the tranquillity she had hoped for was shattered by Marianne's deciding not to eat either. Marianne seemed to sense it every time Laura settled with her cup of coffee, and came along with another pointless query.

'Surely you can deal with that, Marianne? You've been here long enough!' Laura snapped when she could stand no more. Seeing tears glistening in Marianne's eyes, she was immediately contrite, and started to apologise, but Marianne would not listen. She returned to her office, closing the door behind her, and was joined not long afterwards by Brett.

The afternoon lists were under way when Brett appeared and stopped at Laura's desk. 'I must dash away now, I'm already late for the surgery and Dad's being discharged some time, but I'll be back later and I want to talk to you.'

Laura watched his retreating back, shrugging off the ominous tone of his command as just one more hassle in an already difficult day.

It was nearly five when she showed the last patient

136   BASE PRINCIPLES

from the premises and set about tidying the consulting rooms. As she worked, she again sensed Brett's presence in the department and went in search of him, but the office was empty.

Exhausted, she made up her mind that, despite Brett's earlier command, she had no intention of waiting to speak to him. Intending to leave immediately, she was on her way to find Dot when the door of room five opened and Brett came out, closing the door behind him.

'Have you finished now?'

At Laura's nod Brett took her arm. 'I want you to come in and see Marianne. Now.' He was insistent that she stopped whatever she was doing.

'I must tell Dot where I am. I'll be along in a moment.' Laura could not imagine why Brett required her presence, unless Marianne had complained about her. And after the day she had had with the secretary Laura could hardly believe she would have done that. If anybody had reason to complain it was herself. As she looked for Dot, Laura conceded that she should not have snapped at Marianne, but she had apologised almost immediately, even if Marianne had refused to accept it. She couldn't see what could be gained by airing their grievances in front of Brett.

'You get off now, Dot,' she said. 'I've a meeting with Brett and Marianne. I'll let you know if it's anything interesting.'

After Dot had gone, Laura delayed returning to room five as long as she possibly could, and, when she finally plucked up sufficient courage to do so, it was with trepidation that she opened the door.

CHAPTER NINE

MARIANNE had obviously been crying, which fulfilled Laura's worst fears. No doubt she was playing on Brett's sympathies, having named Laura as the villain of the piece.

Defiantly she closed the door behind her and marched across to the only vacant chair.

Brett looked towards Marianne, who nodded, and Laura waited apprehensively for him to speak.

'There's no easy way to say this, Laura——'

'I don't expect there is. Whatever you might have been told, I did apologise for losing my temper, and I don't see what good holding a post-mortem will do.'

'Laura,' Brett was nonplussed, 'what *are* you talking about?'

Hearing exasperation in his tone, Laura realised that she might have misunderstood the situation. But in that case, what on earth was Brett wanting to tell her?

'I don't really know.' She tried to calm the chaotic thoughts tumbling through her mind by asking, 'What did you want to say to me?'

Brett sighed. 'It's about Marianne.'

Laura nodded. She hadn't expected anything else.

'I don't know whether you realise it or not, but I've known Marianne for quite a long time. In fact, I pulled a few strings to get her the screening job.'

'Mm?' Laura could not see for the life of her what this had to do with her.

'I had a very good reason for doing so, Laura. Her father has a mental illness which has disrupted Marianne's home life for several years. The family were on my list at Westleigh, and one of the ways I thought I might be able to help was to get Marianne working in a job that offered stability. It seems to have worked.'

Laura frowned, unable to see why Brett should be telling her all this.

'Obviously Marianne didn't want all and sundry to know, so in fact the only person I confided in was Sister Jones. She promised to keep an eye on Marianne when I was away.'

'But why didn't she tell me when I took over?' Laura was beginning to see why many of her problems had arisen.

'She was happy with the way Marianne was coping, and, having discussed it, they both decided it would be better to leave things as they were, especially as Mr Barker's problem appeared to be in a quiescent phase.'

'But—but surely she didn't expect that to last indefinitely?'

'No, but she hoped I'd be back before trouble brewed. As it happens, I was—just. Unfortunately he entered a manic phase the moment I set foot back in Westleigh. Perhaps it was fortunate it didn't happen before, because Mr Barker has a pronounced distrust of the medical profession, apart from me. Hence my frequent visits to the Barker household.'

Laura knew by his expression that Brett was trying to tell her more than he was actually saying, but she was already finding it a problem to adjust to this totally unexpected version of events. 'So how is Mr Barker now?'

'That's the present problem. Not good. The night I let you down his condition deteriorated, and I couldn't leave him until I'd managed to get him admitted to a psychiatric hospital where he could do no damage to himself or to anybody else. As you know, it's difficult to keep anybody there these days, and he was discharged back into the community the following week.'

Marianne gave a pronounced sob as Brett continued, 'Poor old Marianne's been having a rough time since then, and last night was the final straw. Her mother rang to say he'd taken his whole bottle of tablets that afternoon and had been admitted to the General.'

'I'm sorry, I'd no idea.' Laura was appalled to learn of Marianne's problems.

'No, but I'm sure you can imagine the difficult position I was in when Marianne didn't want anyone to know.'

Taking another tissue, Marianne dabbed at her eyes. 'I'm so ashamed I just hate anybody knowing my problems. Brett took me to his church, thinking it would be a help if I could talk things over with the vicar, but it didn't work—I think he was afraid of Dad. I can't leave Mum to cope alone if Dad comes home, but if I take even more time off work Brett says you'll have to be told.'

Marianne's tearful explanation caused Laura a stab of anguish that she had not been more understanding about the girl's past absences, although deep in her heart she knew she had only been doing her job. If only Sister Jones had passed the information on, she would have understood.

Laura's reverie was broken by Brett explaining gently, 'The General want to discharge him home again this evening, and I can't see any way of stopping it.'

Noting his helpless expression and how tired he looked, Laura felt desperately sorry for him. He had become deeply involved with the Barkers' problems, because he cared too much. And all the time his Hippocratic Oath had prevented him sharing the problem. Laura was embarrassed to recall how she had questioned his ethics on more than one occasion. She felt her heart swell with respect for him.

Suddenly everything began to fall into place for her. The number of times she had overheard one of them referring to a meeting the previous evening, and even last night, when Marianne had been so upset and Laura had heard Brett say he'd done all he could, she had wanted nothing more than her father readmitted to the psychiatric hospital. Laura felt ashamed of her resentment, although it was clear how her misconceptions had arisen.

Marianne was by this time weeping openly, while Brett looked on helplessly. Guessing intuitively that the way to help them both was to attempt to restore the situation to a semblance of normality, Laura said brightly, 'Can I get you both some coffee?'

'It's a kind offer, Laura, but I think I ought to get Marianne down to the hospital as soon as possible. We arranged to meet her mother there.' The relief that flashed across Brett's features told Laura she had done the right thing.

She nodded. 'I understand. I'll leave you two to get off while I clear up. Is there anything urgent outstanding on your desk, Marianne?'

Sniffing, the girl replied, 'I don't think so, thanks.'

As Brett helped Marianne to her feet, he turned to Laura. 'Thanks for being a good listener. Will you be here much longer?'

She shook her head. 'I'm off home at the first possible moment.'

She watched him biting his lip as if undecided what to do, then, shrugging, he led Marianne along the corridor.

Puzzled, Laura switched off all the lights and hastened downstairs to change. Brett had obviously wanted to say something more to her, but had felt unable to in Marianne's presence. Well, he knew her telephone number; it was up to him if he wanted to make contact.

Throughout the long, wet journey home, Laura mulled over the events of the evening. Recalling Brett's reaction to her explanation for calling a taxi the previous evening, together with his obvious interest in her the night before, she began to recognise that she might have made a complete fool of herself. Was that what Brett had wanted to tell her before he went off with Marianne? Had it been Marianne's idea to explain the true situation? Or had Brett an ulterior motive for persuading her to do so? If only she could believe what her heart wanted to hear, but on reflection Laura knew he had merely explained his support for Marianne, nothing more. Her mind in a whirl, she walked slowly, and, arriving home cold and wet, was more than grateful for the casserole her mother had prepared.

It was when they were all part way through their meal that her mother dropped the bombshell.

'What do you think of Brett's offer?'

'Brett's offer? What on earth do you mean?'

'Didn't he see you this evening? He said he'd get back to the Wellstead before you left.'

Suspiciously, Laura enquired again, 'What offer?'

'He's arranged for Dad to have his first hip replacement next week at the Wellstead. Isn't that great?'

'And who's paying?' Although Laura tried to keep the mounting suspicion from her voice, she knew her expression probably gave her away.

'Why, he is, of course. He wouldn't take no for an answer.' Her mother was obviously delighted by the prospect. 'Said it was the least he could do in the circumstances.'

'What circumstances?' Laura had given up any attempt to either hide her resentment or finish her meal. 'Mum, do you realise just how much that's going to cost him?'

'Yes, he told us.'

Her father, who had said nothing until that moment, took Laura's hand. 'You're not happy about this, are you, love?'

'What do you think, Dad? I hardly know him, and don't find him the easiest person to work with. Don't get me wrong, there's nothing I'd like more than for you to be free from pain, but I don't understand his motives, especially not mentioning it to me this morning.' Making a determined attempt not to allow her father to see how angry she was, Laura realised she had failed miserably.

Patting her hand, he tried to reassure her, 'I can understand that, Laura; it could make things difficult for you.'

Feeling there was no way she could dash her father's

hopes now Brett had raised them, Laura pushed back her chair and hugged her father.

'Don't worry about it. I'll have a chat with him tomorrow. I'm probably not seeing this in perspective. I just wish he'd felt able to tell me himself.'

Despite her exhaustion, she spent a restless night, dreaming first of her father being back to his old self again, then Brett's reaction to her flinging the offer back at him. She awoke in a cold sweat in the early hours, and, unable to sleep again, tried to work out if there was any way she and her mother could raise the money themselves, but she knew it was a forlorn hope.

Brett was not expected in the department the next morning, and she wondered where she should contact him if he did not put in an appearance, for there was no way she could delay discussing his offer. As she set out for the Wellstead earlier than usual, it occurred to Laura that Marianne would know his whereabouts. She hoped their working relationship would be much improved following the previous evening's disclosures.

Arriving in the department, she discovered that the one thing she hadn't taken into consideration had occurred. Marianne was absent from work, and the message awaiting Laura said she was unable to say when she would be back. Until a temporary secretary could be engaged, it was going to mean a lot more work for the nursing staff.

She was thankful to find the notes prepared for the day's sessions, but no lists, so that was her first task.

She was only halfway through when she heard footsteps in the corridor and sensed immediately that it was Brett. Unprepared for such an early meeting, Laura rose from Marianne's desk feeling flustered.

'Morning, Laura.' Brett came striding across the office to meet her.' 'Sorry about this, but I've suggested at least a week off for Marianne.'

Anxiously chewing at her bottom lip, Laura avoided meeting his eyes as she answered, 'That's understandable.'

'Good. I hoped you'd see it that way. I'm sorry I had to spring the whole sordid business on to you so suddenly last night, but Marianne wanted me to tell you while she was still there. She knew she'd been impossible recently and was hoping for absolution.'

Trying to recall how she had reacted, Laura murmured, 'I hope I made the right noises.'

'You acted as if there was no problem, and that was just what Marianne needed. I'm grateful to you, Laura.'

Detecting a tremor in his voice, Laura forced herself to meet his gaze as she summoned up the courage to broach the subject of her father.

'Brett, I. . .' She stopped abruptly to allow him to finish the sentence he started at the same moment.

'Laura, I do apologise for not telling you about my offer to your father myself, but, as you know, I didn't get a chance yesterday evening.'

Defiantly, Laura replied, 'I should have thought you'd have asked my opinion *before* you started raising his hopes in the way you did. It's obvious we can't accept charity on that scale.'

Brett slowly lowered himself into the seat beside Marianne's desk and drummed a tattoo with his fingers. When he eventually spoke, his voice was cold. 'Has it not occurred to you that that's the reason I approached your father first? I knew your pride would never allow you to accept help from me, but this arrangement is purely between him and myself. I liked him immensely at our first meeting and I was sure he would accept my offer in the spirit it was made.'

'Which was?' Laura's tone was sharp.

'I didn't see why he should go on suffering, when there was something I could do about it. That, in case you've forgotten, is the basis of the oath I took on qualifying.'

'It didn't say you had to finance his cure.' Laura felt she was rapidly losing the argument and snapped out a reply she regretted almost immediately.

Brett, realising her vulnerability, pressed home his argument. 'I spent a lot more than a hip operation costs to help the people of Sudan, and no one complained about accepting charity then. I can't see what the difference is.'

Laura sighed heavily. 'We're not in the same situation as the Sudanese. We——'

'Just have too much pride,' Brett interrupted. 'Personally I can't see the difference. Both need relief from suffering, and as I'm in the lucky position to be able to help I don't see what there is to complain about. Anyway, I thought you'd be glad to know that some of my father's ill-gotten gains from the Leys Estate were being used to help other people!'

The lop-sided grin that lightened his angry features told Laura he realised there was no way she could deny that premise. 'C'mon—fair's fair. You helped my father, now let me help yours.'

Not for the first time Laura felt herself trapped in a corner by his skilful use of words. And yet perversely she felt a wave of relief sweep over her that, after all, she needn't cause her father further heartache. Brett's uncompromising way of putting his offer meant there was no way they could not accept it.

Longing to show her gratitude in a more tangible way, she tentatively laid her hand on his arm. 'What can I say but thank you very much? I'm sorry——'

However, Brett rudely interrupted her attempt at humility. 'I'm not looking for your thanks. It has nothing to do with you. The offer was made to your father.'

Laura's blood ran cold at the coolness in his voice. She couldn't believe he could mean what he had just said, but when she met his impassive stare she knew it was true.

He intercepted her surreptitious glance towards the office clock. 'I won't delay you any further, because I'm late as it is for my surgery.'

Feeling dismissed by his total indifference, Laura turned to leave the office, but he laid a delaying hand on her arm. 'But not until you tell me you won't obstruct this operation.' Irritably, Laura attempted to pull her arm free. 'I mean it, Laura.' Brett's features resumed a determined expression to match his tone, and he tightened his grip, sending an unexpected sensation hurtling through her veins.

'You don't leave me much option—I can't disappoint my father now and you know it.'

He nodded, his face alight with satisfaction. Releasing his grip, he murmured, 'I'll get the arrangements under way. See you,' and was gone before she had a chance to discover exactly when he was referring to.

As she left the office Laura was relieved to see Pam coming on duty. 'Marianne won't be in today, so I'm rather behind. Can you check the rooms while I finish the paperwork?'

'Is Marianne ill?' Pam queried. 'She wasn't in a particularly good mood yesterday, was she?'

'She probably felt under the weather then.' Laura hurried away, hoping Pam would ask no further questions until she had had time to work out a convincing explanation.

The day continued as it had started, and Laura never seemed to catch up. She had a short breathing-space at eleven, and took the opportunity to ring home and reassure her father that the operation plans were going ahead.

'Yes, dear, we know,' her mother greeted the news. 'Brett called to take some blood about ten minutes ago. Dad is to be admitted on Sunday and will probably have the op Monday.'

'But Mr Hawkins is still away?' Laura couldn't work out how Brett could have made the arrangements.

'Yes,' her mother agreed, 'but apparently he had another hip planned for Monday and the chap has cried off, so Dad will take his place. We'll never be able to thank Brett enough, will we?'

Laura sighed regretfully. 'No, we won't. I must go now, Mum. See you later.'

The remainder of Friday passed in a blur. It seemed she was never able to stop for even a moment, though, as she changed out of her uniform to go home, she admitted to herself that it had been a good thing. Her thoughts were too confused to give them only part of her attention. When she tried to work out her feelings, she wanted to be able to think of nothing else, and she

knew she might as well put off that luxury until she was
in bed.

Her mother was in high spirits when Laura arrived
home, in contrast to her father's subdued demeanour.

'Are you sure it's not going to cause problems for
you, love?' he asked the moment Mrs Pennington had
bustled off to the kitchen to dish up the meal.

Laura nodded. 'Yes, Dad, I had a long talk with
Brett this morning and he set my mind at rest.'

'Good. I won't deny I'd be disappointed now if it
didn't go ahead, but your happiness means as much to
me.'

'I know that, Dad. But you can have both. OK?'
Laura kissed him lightly on his bald spot.

'I hope you mean that, because I like Brett, and I
think your happiness could be tied up with him.'

'Oh, Dad, don't be silly! We just work together.'

'Hm. But how many other of your colleagues have
bothered to come and help us? No, you just wait and
see, I know what I'm talking about.'

Laura gave him a hug. 'I do love you, Dad, and
you'll be the first to know if you're right.'

Her mother came in with the serving dishes at that
moment, enquiring, 'Right about what?'

'We were guessing what you're producing for
dinner.'

'Go on, you old silly!' Mrs Pennington turned to her
husband fondly. 'I told you this morning we were
having boiled gammon.'

'Why, so you did.' Mr Pennington winked conspiratorially at Laura and the subject was dropped.

'Brett's offered to take Dad into the hospital on
Sunday. He said he hoped we'd both be able to go with

him.' Katherine Pennington dropped her information into the conversation as she was clearing the plates away.

'Didn't you tell him we could manage?' Laura was annoyed by her mother's passive acceptance. 'He's not had much free time this week as it is.'

'Of course I told him, but he seemed to want to do it, so I didn't argue.'

Laura had to accept the arrangement, which, added to her earlier confused thoughts, resulted in yet another couple of disturbed nights. So by the time Brett came to collect them on Sunday afternoon she was no nearer sorting out her emotions than she had been on Friday morning when Brett had left her with his recriminations ringing in her ears.

'We're all ready. Would you like a cup of tea first?' Laura cringed at what she considered excessive servility from her mother.

'No, I told the hospital we'd be there before five, so I think we'll get straight off.'

Laura and Brett helped Rob Pennington into the front passenger-seat, then Laura joined her mother in the back. She was thankful for the non-stop stream of conversation her mother kept up, as it prevented her from having to think of something to say to Brett.

A good hour had passed by the time they settled Rob into his room, and, when Laura's mother appeared reluctant to leave, Brett suggested, 'How about having an evening meal with your husband and I'll take Laura for a bite to eat? We'll come back to collect you later.'

'That's a good idea.' Eager to encourage Laura's and Brett's friendship, Katherine Pennington didn't give a second thought to the suggestion until they were leaving. 'Laura, will they serve me a meal with your father?'

'Of course they will, Mum. I'll order it on the way out. They'll put it on the final bill.' Then, seeing a golden opportunity to tease her mother about Brett, Laura added in a sudden fit of devilment, 'You'll have to reimburse Brett for it, as it'll be in the grand total!'

'What a thing to say to your mother!' Brett chided as they waited for the lift to arrive.

Laura thought she detected a hint of amusement at the corner of his lips, and her hazel eyes sparkled as she feigned remorse. 'She's sung your praises so often and so loudly this weekend that I couldn't resist it. Don't worry, Dad'll tell her I was only stringing her along.'

They climbed into the lift and Brett pushed the ground floor button. 'I'm very pleased to hear it. I thought it was one more manifestation of your fixation with finance.'

Already unsure where she stood with Brett, Laura did not know whether he was joking or genuinely criticising. So she was grateful that the lift stopped at that moment, and she did not need to give an immediate answer. However, a quick search of his features was no help, revealing only a deadpan expression that gave her no clue to his emotions.

Chastened, she didn't speak until they reached the car.

'Where are we going?'

'Depends.' Brett unlocked the doors of his Mercedes and they both climbed in.

'Depends on what?' Laura fastened her seatbelt.

'On how you're going to behave.' He flashed her a look of amused tolerance, then, turning his attention to the controls of the car, started up the engine.

Indignantly Laura protested, 'What do you mean? I don't behave badly.'

When he merely raised his eyebrows in disbelief, she began to get annoyed. 'If you find my behaviour so disagreeable, you can take me back to the hospital now.'

Brett glanced towards her and removing a hand from the steering-wheel, patted her knee. 'I told you how attractive I find you when you're angry. I can't resist it.'

Laura digested his reply thoughtfully. 'So it's not *my* behaviour that's the problem?'

He gave a deep chuckle. '*Touché!*' He drove in silence for a little way before adding, 'I thought we might get something to eat at the Carpenters. If that would be to your liking? If we eat in the bar we should be through in plenty of time to collect your mother from the hospital.'

No longer sure how to cope with Brett's banter, Laura replied demurely, 'That sounds very pleasant.'

When he once again directed his glance towards her, she saw his lips twitching with amusement. Suspecting that he was laughing at her, she resigned herself to never understanding this man who was doing so much for her family.

As he pulled into the Carpenters' car park, he smiled at Laura. 'Well, how about me giving you a penny for them?'

'For what?'

'Those very deep and serious thoughts that are marring your unfurrowed brow.'

To hide her confusion, Laura retorted, 'I'm wondering what we're going to eat. I'm starving!'

Brett laughed. 'Is that all? How disappointing! I hoped you were about to divulge your innermost secrets.'

Laura joined in the laughter and, opening the passenger door, jumped out into the car park.

Brett came round and, taking her hand, murmured, 'You're shying away again. Relax. I'm not trying to intimidate you—quite the contrary. Surely I've made that clear by now?'

Laura smiled up at him through eyelashes damp with emotion. 'We've known each other such a short time, Brett. Apart from your generosity, I know so little about you.'

Tucking her hand round his waist, he leant closer and kissed her lightly on the lips before murmuring, 'We'll have to remedy that. I feel I know you so well that I expect you to feel the same.'

Laura allowed the delighted tremor that shook her body to subside before she said, 'I meant it, Brett. We'll never be able to repay you for all you're doing for us.'

Brett smiled as he replied, 'I can think of many ways *you* are going to do that.' The seductive tone of his voice left Laura in no doubt of his meaning, and her lurching heart felt as if it were dropping through her empty stomach.

Momentarily too affected to speak, she shyly glanced up from under silky lashes. Finding herself unable to tear her eyes away from the hooded sensuality of his gaze, she moved towards him as he encircled her with two firm arms.

When he eventually released her the sensation of numbing loss caused her to stagger slightly.

He was immediately contrite. 'This is no way to treat a lady! You can continue your show of gratitude after we've eaten.' Pulling her close to his side, he laughed contentedly and pushed open the door of the bar. When he went to look for a menu, Laura tried to sort out her confusion. To say he hadn't made an instant impression on her would be wrong, even though initially it had not been particularly favourable. However, his personality had won her over to be one of his band of admirers, and perhaps that was her trouble. She craved for his undivided attention, and she still wasn't sure that was what he was offering.

'Found one at last.' Brett handed her a leather-bound menu. 'I'll get you a drink while you decide. What'll it be?'

'A dry Martini, please.' Laura perused the menu inattentively, her thoughts still centred on Brett.

'Decided?' He returned with the drinks ready to order the food before he joined her at the corner table.

'Sorry, Brett, I was miles away.' She hastily picked out a home-baked ham dish and handed him the menu.

'I'll join you, I think.' Making his way back to the bar through the rapidly increasing throng, Brett disappeared from view, giving Laura a chance to reflect again on her reaction to him. Recalling his accusations of her fixation with finance, she hoped he didn't think her sudden response was solely gratitude. Nothing could be further from the truth, and if that was what he believed she must somehow convince him that his ideas about her were totally wrong.

CHAPTER TEN

'A GOOD job we arrived when we did—there isn't a free table in the place.' Brett had returned from the bar and taken his seat beside Laura. 'Now, what would you like to know about me?'

Her cheeks were hot as she stammered, 'I—I d-don't. . . There's nothing specific I want to know. I just feel that because we don't really know one another we may have got the wrong impression.'

Brett raised his eyebrows quizzically. 'And what is your impression of me?'

Unflinching, she met his frank gaze. 'Well, although I admire your philanthropy, I think you're more than used to getting your own way, your path in life having been smoothed by your family's wealth.'

'Ho, that's certainly telling me! I think I need notice before answering those charges——'

'I wasn't accusing you of anything,' Laura interrupted hurriedly, 'I was just stating the facts as I saw them.' Aware that her candour had probably not improved the situation, she was relieved to see the waitress arriving with their plates of ham coated lightly with a cheese sauce. 'This looks good.'

They ate in silence, but every time Laura raised her eyes she found Brett watching her closely, as if trying to weigh her up.

When they had both finished, he pushed back his

plate and, resting his chin in his hands, asked, 'Another drink? And what else to eat?'

'I'd just like coffee, if that's all right by you.'

'Suits me fine. I'll struggle through this crush and order it. Sure I can't tempt you to one of those delicious-looking sweets?'

Laura nodded. 'No, thanks. They do look tempting, but, having had roast beef at lunchtime, I mustn't.'

As she was speaking Brett's eyes appraised her approvingly. 'I can't see why not, but I'll bow to your wishes. Coffee it shall be.'

This time his absence gave her the opportunity to mull over the insistent thought dominating her tumultuous mind. Brett was coming to mean too much to her. The sense of comfortable belonging she had experienced even during their companionable silence was a sure indication that her heart was becoming far too susceptible.

Before she could could decide how to lower the tension she felt between them, Brett returned with the coffee and seated himself close to her. 'Now, let's discover what wrong impression you suspect I have of you.'

His eyes darkened visibly as his intent gaze searched her face for an answer. To gain time, Laura sipped her coffee slowly before stammering, 'I—er——I——You keep mentioning my obsession with money. I don't have one.'

'You don't?' Brett's eyebrows lifted cynically. 'I can assure you I'm not usually the one who brings the subject up.' He drank his coffee slowly, watching her over the rim of the cup.

'But you don't understand. You. . .'

'I'll be waiting.'

As she set off for work, Laura pictured her mother finding nothing to occupy herself after the years she had devoted to her husband, and felt a wave of sadness sweep over her at not having been in a position to give more help.

She was in early, but, with full lists for both Brett and Peggy Andrews, and Marianne still away, she did not have a spare moment to wonder how her father was faring.

It was just after ten when the nurse who had accompanied her father down to the theatre stopped by to let Laura know. From then on, Laura found it difficult to concentrate. When she handed Brett the wrong notes for the second time, he led her gently to the coffee-room.

'Sit down and leave things to Pam for once. He'll no doubt be fine, despite all the possibilities for disaster that you're imagining.'

Laura took the mug of coffee he offered. 'Thanks. Knowing too much can be as much of a problem as not knowing enough. But you're right—I shouldn't be thinking of all the things that can go wrong!'

'I've only one more patient before lunch and your dad should be back in the ward by then, so we'll pop up and visit him.'

Brett was as good as his word, and it was just after one when they discovered that Rob Pennington wasn't yet back from the recovery-room. Laura clutched at Brett's arm, her face drained of colour. 'Do you think something's gone wrong?'

'Of course I don't. You know as well as I do that they probably haven't had a moment to transfer him.'

Once again Laura was grateful for Brett's support. She knew she was probably overreacting, but when it was your own relative who was concerned the situation was very different.

At that moment the lift doors clanged back and the stretcher bearing her father appeared. Laura leant over him and touched his forehead. He opened his eyes and smiled at her.

'All well?' she mouthed to the recovery-room nurse.

'No problems at all. Now I suggest you get off for a bite to eat while we get him settled in bed.'

Laura did as she was told, stopping on the way to convey the good news to her mother.

'Tell her I'll bring her in to see him this evening if she likes.' Brett was listening with amusement to Laura's reassurance.

As they ate lunch Laura said, 'I'll come in with Mum.'

He shook his head. 'I don't think you should. You can see him briefly before you leave, but he probably won't feel like visitors, and the rest will do you good.'

Laura arrived home in time to have an early meal with her mother before Brett arrived. However, just before he was due the telephone rang.

'Is that Laura Pennington? This is the Westleigh receptionist. Dr Farraday is sorry, but he's been called out on an emergency. He asked me to arrange for a taxi for your mother and it's on its way now, all paid for. Dr Farraday said he'd be in touch with you later.'

Laura did as Brett had suggested and spent the evening catching up on her mending and letter writing. Her mother was soon back, leaving her husband to a good night's sleep.

She delayed going to bed as long as possible, sure Brett would either call or telephone. When she hadn't heard from him by half-past eleven, she realised what a fool she was, and, making a cup of tea, took herself up to bed. But not to sleep. Her mind wouldn't allow that as she absorbed the unpalatable truth that Brett hadn't meant a word he'd said the previous evening. He was not even interested enough to keep his promise.

Exhausted, Laura dragged herself to work the next morning, allowing herself one tiny ray of hope that before he began his morning surgery Brett might, as he had done before, call in at the clinic to explain.

However, that glimmer was soon extinguished. Laura carried out her routine tasks in the deserted department, each one rubbing salt into her wounds as it reminded her of Brett. Dispirited, she doubted if it would be possible to work with him in the future, when every thought caused such a bitter pain. Yet for her father's sake she could not just dismiss him from her life, but from now on she would ensure that there was no opportunity for any more amorous advances he might feel obliged to make.

The arrival of the first appointment at the same time as Pam allowed her to push the thoughts to the back of her mind. Pam took Mr Taplow to perform an ECG on him, while Laura looked for the morning's notes, as yet another temporary secretary had not put in an appearance after only one day with them.

Having assembled the list, Laura quickly rang the ward, and was relieved to discover her father was progressing well. As she replaced the receiver a very subdued Marianne entered the office. The black rings around her bloodshot eyes gave a clear indication of her emotional state; not only had she been crying recently, but she couldn't have slept properly for nights.

Laura crossed to greet her, slipping her arm around her shoulders. 'Whatever are you doing here, Marianne? I wasn't expecting you back yet.'

Marianne tried to stifle a sob. 'I thought I'd be better back at work—help me forget.'

Laura led her over to the easy chair. 'Has the situation deteriorated? Where's your father now?'

'Back in the General, but this time they're not going to let him out. He'll be transferred directly to the psychiatric hospital.'

'Oh, Marianne, I am sorry!' Seeing the distress in Marianne's eyes, Laura asked no more questions. 'Would you like some coffee?' Marianne nodded, and listlessly started to sort through some of the papers on her desk.

When Laura returned, she found the girl frowning over the appointment diary.

'Shall I cancel all these, or can you find someone else to do the extra smear clinic this afternoon?'

'Cancel them? I don't understand. Won't Brett be here?'

Marianne clapped a hand to her mouth. 'Oh—I thought you'd know. What a fool I am—you'd better sit down and I'll explain.' Sighing deeply, she continued, 'I don't believe this. Especially after Brett insisted I explain the reason he's been helping me. I thought someone would have let you know.'

'Brett insisted? But I thought you—I thought it was because you needed some time off.'

Compressing her lips tightly, Marianne shook her head. 'That was part of it, but it was not only for my sake that he wanted you to know the whole story. He was worried that his support for me was causing misunderstanding between you. He wanted to set the record straight so that you and he—and now this has to happen.' The tears glistening in Marianne's eyes overflowed.

Unable to take in the implication of the secretary's words, Laura felt bewildered. 'What's happened? Has something happened to Brett?' Grasping Marianne's arm, she pleaded, 'For goodness' sake tell me!'

'Dad went berserk again last night. Brett came over to help and Dad took a swipe at him. He caught him off balance and Brett fell, hitting his head on the marble fireplace. Oh, Laura, he's been unconscious since. He's next door, in Intensive Care.'

Laura bit hard on her knuckles to prevent herself crying out. All the time she had been thinking dreadful things about Brett, he had been fighting for his life. Her confused mind still unable to take it all in, she reacted with surprise when Marianne urged her to go and see him as soon as possible, but she did not argue.

'I'll go now, Marianne; Pam can hold the fort.'

Laura sped along the corridor and, without divulging Marianne's involvement, briefly explained the situation to Pam, emphasising the need to check Brett's availability for that week's lists.

As she arrived at the door of the intensive care unit, the first person she saw was Brett's father. 'Hello, lass, I thought you'd be up when the hospital let you know.' Despite his sombre expression, Laura was relieved not to detect hopelessness in his voice.

'But they didn't—I mean, it was Marianne. . .' Laura stopped her meaningless chatter and asked the question that she was afraid to voice, 'How is Brett?'

'Still out like a light. The doctors can't find too much wrong with him, so they hope he might come round today.' The fatigue on Bram Farraday's face showed plainly the anxious night he must have spent at his son's bedside. 'But you never can tell with these cases, can you? It's a waiting game. If you want to pop in and see him, he's in the first bed.'

Laura entered the unit with trepidation, fearful of what she might find. Lying on his side, Brett was covered by a single sheet, an unusual pallor obvious despite his tan. If it hadn't been for the monitor blipping away at his bedside, she could have imagined he was in nothing more than a deep sleep.

Taking his hand, she leant over and kissed his forehead. 'Hello, Brett. It's me, Laura.' His features showed not a flicker of interest, so Laura continued to chat quietly, telling him how well her father was doing and stressing how much they needed him back at the screening centre.

'Don't forget we've got all those extra sessions booked for you.' Laura's eyes were moist with tears as her nonsensical chatter made no impression on the inert figure, but she continued for a little while longer, knowing brain stimulation by familiar voices was thought to penetrate the unconscious mind.

'I'll have to get back to work now, Brett, but I'll be up to see you later.' His continuing lack of response made Laura appreciate what years of training had failed to do—just how difficult it was to hold a one-sided conversation at the bedside.

The young sister checking his monitor smiled. 'If you want to get back, we can always call you if necessary.'

As Laura left the room, the sister followed her. 'Don't worry too much—there doesn't seem to be any permanent damage, and he should soon start to recover consciousness.'

Laura nodded, relieved to know that from now on she would be informed of any change in Brett's condition. Knowing it was essential to rearrange his clinics for the rest of the week, she made her way slowly back to the screening centre, her anxiety at his condition tempered by relief that he hadn't deliberately let her down.

Marianne must have been waiting anxiously for her return, as the moment Laura turned into the corridor she was besieged by questions.

'How was he? Is he conscious yet? Do you think he'll be all right?' Marianne's tearful inquisition did not allow Laura a chance to answer. 'Are Mr and Mrs Farraday there?'

'Steady on!' Laura took Marianne's arm. 'Come along to the office and I'll try and answer your questions one by one.' And perhaps ask a few of my own, she added silently.

Marianne sniffed loudly, and Laura nipped into the nearest consulting-room and grabbed a box of tissues.

Leading the red-eyed girl to the easy-chair, she seated herself at the secretary's desk. 'Now, first of all there seems to be no change in Brett's condition. He's not conscious, but at the moment no one seems unduly worried, and his father is with him.' Pausing to make sure Marianne had absorbed all she had said so far, Laura added gently, 'As to the final outcome, nobody can really guess at the moment, but Sister told me the doctors were quite optimistic.'

'But if he dies?' As she finished speaking, Marianne let out a strangled sob and dissolved into tears, forcing Laura to face the possibility she was trying to ignore.

'Look, Marianne, getting into this state is going to help no one. Now, have you been to see Brett?'

Marianne shook her head forcefully. 'No, I couldn't.'

Laura placed an arm gently around the secretary's shoulders. 'Yes, you could, it'll set your mind at rest. We'll go up together later.' She was amazed at the calm way she was helping Marianne to come to terms with Brett's injury, when inside she was screaming. No doubt it had something to do with her training.

When the secretary's sobs at last abated, Laura suggested, 'Rearranging Brett's sessions is one way you can do something to help. But before you do that I'll see if Peggy Andrews can possibly help us out.' She rose from her chair, saying, 'I'll ring her from my desk, then you can get yourself sorted out in here.'

Picking up the diary, she left the office with a feeling of relief. Drained of all emotion, she longed to get away to try and piece together her jumbled thoughts.

As she dialled Peggy's number, she recalled Marianne's emphasising that it was at Brett's insistence she told Laura of her home problems. The thought sent her heart leaping as she recalled Brett's declaration of love.

'Wellstead 987542.' Peggy's voice at the other end of the line roused Laura from her reverie.

'Hi, Peggy, it's Laura. Sorry to disturb you, but we have a problem. I know you said you hadn't a spare moment, but I just wondered if there was any way you

Marianne's confirmation of her own conclusions—a state of being that would have transported her into ecstasy had it not been for Brett's present condition. As it was, the moment she finished her light snack she made her way up to the intensive care unit with a cold dread that Brett might never recover completely.

This time she found only the ward sister with him. She rose as Laura approached the bed. 'He's improving all the time. I'll leave you to it. Give a shout if you need me.'

Exultant at the good news, but anxious not to offend Brett's parents, Laura asked, 'Is his father still around? I don't want them to think I'm monopolising him.'

'No, he's gone for something to eat and will be back later with his wife.'

Laura settled beside Brett and again started to chatter to him, and even plucked up the courage to tell him she loved him. This time he showed some kind of response to nearly every word, occasionally muttering an answer, though Laura found it difficult to decipher the words.

'He's going on a treat, isn't he?' Proudly, as if Brett were recovering by his efforts, Mr Farraday had returned to the other side of the bed, while his wife hovered in the doorway.

'Yes, he's responding well. I should think he'll soon be back to normal.' Laura left them alone with Brett while she visited her own father and explained the situation to her mother, who had just arrived.

Her prophecy was nearly correct. Within twenty-four hours Brett had moved into a single room and was seated in an armchair, apparently the picture of health. But he was as cantankerous as recuperating head injury patients tended to be. Not having had a chance to visit him all day Wednesday, Laura looked in before going home and found the neurologist visiting. She arrived just in time to hear Brett demand to know why he could not go home.

'I think we need you under observation for a little while longer, my lad. Just bide your impatience. I'll be in tomorrow afternoon. You tell him, m'dear, he's better off staying here at the moment.' He closed the door behind him.

It was the first time Laura had been alone with Brett since he regained his faculties, and she felt embarrassed, unsure what he might recall of her chatter.

'You look much better tonight, Brett, very different——'

Interrupting her, Brett tugged irritably at his pyjama collar. 'Well, I'm not. I'm just the old difficult Brett. What are you doing here anyway?'

Laura tried every way she could to humour him. She told him how well her father was progressing, and how Peggy Andrews was coping with his work, but nothing seemed to please him, and in the end she left disconsolately to visit her father instead. After Marianne's confirmation of her suspicions such antagonism was the last thing Laura had expected from Brett. She had looked forward to misunderstandings being a thing of the past. As it was, she left his room feeling depressed and hurt that he could not even be civil to her.

On her way out, Laura popped her head round the office door to say, 'I've left Brett on his own—I thought you probably ought to know.'

The relief sister laughed ruefully. 'Why? Do you

think he'll attempt to escape in his pyjamas? He's like a bear with a sore head, isn't he?'

Laura nodded. 'I suppose that's the problem, a sore head.'

'I'm afraid so. I used to work with him at the General, and I go in there expecting his usual pleasant manner and am taken aback every time by his response. Anyway, I'll pop along and try to persuade him back to bed for the night.'

Laura saw no point in returning to Brett's room before she left the hospital with her mother, and she spent a sleepless night regretting the impulse that had made her bare her soul to the semi-conscious Brett.

So she was not particularly sympathetic on Thursday morning to receive a telephone call from Sister Grimes. 'As soon as you've got a free moment, Laura, do you think you could come up and see Brett? He's demanding to see you immediately.'

Thankful that it was impossible to go at that moment, she went up to Brett's room in her own good time. Expecting him to be alone, she was surprised to find his parents, Sister Grimes and the neurologist ranged around the room, in various hostile stances.

'Come in, Laura.' Mr Farraday looked relieved to see her.

'Brett is demanding to go home to his own place— this morning if possible.' Ruth Grimes's tone was placatory, and Laura wondered why. 'He's been told it's not a good idea for him to be alone in his flat all day. His mother——'

'Stop talking about me as if I'm not here!' Brett glared round the room. 'I'm not prepared to be smothered by my mother, and that's final. If Laura won't come and look after me I'll get a nurse from one of the agencies.'

Startled, Laura began, 'What——?'

'That's why I asked you to come up.' Ruth's glance appealed to Laura not to upset Brett further. 'He wants you to look after him.'

'But Brett, how can I? I can't neglect my work.'

'You can take some leave.'

Laura sighed, imagining Mr Edwards's reaction to her demanding immediate annual leave. 'I suppose I could ask, but——'

'I hope you're not going to say your father needs you, because we both know he's well looked after here. My need is greater.' When Laura hesitated, Brett snapped, 'Well, don't you want to look after me?'

There was nothing she would have liked more than to look after the charming man who had told her he loved her only a few nights before, but she was not at all sure that nursing such a grouch was a prospect she relished. It could spell the end of their relationship even before it had started. However, she appeased him by saying, 'Of course I want to, but I do have a job to do.'

'Well, go and arrange some time off.'

'I'll see what I can do.' Laura was sure it was not going to be easy. However, it was all arranged with a minimum of fuss. Mr Coates, the neurologist, accompanied her down to the director's office, and, having heard the tale, Mr Edwards gave Laura a week off with the option of further time if necessary.

Before returning to Brett's room, Laura slipped along to her own department and told Pam what was happening. 'Mr Edwards is borrowing a nurse from next door, so I'm leaving you and Dot to run the place for a few days.'

She then searched out Marianne and explained the situation.

'I *am* glad you're going with him. I'll help Dot and Pam as much as I can.' The knowledge that Brett was obviously on the mend had boosted Marianne's morale.

'You know where I am, Marianne, if things deteriorate at home—ring any time.'

'Thanks, Sister—for everything.'

Laura left the department still questioning whether she was doing the right thing. Brett had hardly uttered a civil word in the past couple of days, and yet he appeared to want her alone to look after him. It didn't make sense, but then nothing about Brett ever had.

She returned to his room to find his father waiting to drive them home. As she packed his belongings, his mother fussed until Brett became quite irritable.

She, in her turn, appeared hurt by his irritability and refused to accompany them to Brett's flat.

'I'll do some shopping instead.'

The moment they were in the car Brett rested his head back and heaved a deep sigh. 'Now you see why I didn't want to go home. My mother would drive me up the wall and down again with her fussing!'

Arriving at a modern block of purpose-built flats overlooking the downs, Laura helped Brett inside while his father carried the bags.

'I'll leave you in peace to sort yourselves out, but ring if you want anything.'

'Thanks, Mr Farraday.' Laura took the bags from him at the front door. 'But don't forget you're still supposed to be convalescing.'

'Bram, please. And don't you worry about me, I'm as strong as a horse.'

'Thanks for the offer, then.' Unsure what she might find in the flat, Laura gratefully said she would be in touch.

The moment he was inside his own flat Brett appeared to relax. 'Put those bags over there and come and sit beside me,' he ordered. As Laura surveyed the obvious bachelor pad, Brett settled on a black leather two-seater settee.

'But wouldn't you be better in bed——?' Laura perched on the edge of the seat beside him and took his hand.

'Don't you start!' he snarled.

Worried by the sight of tension building up in his shoulders, she hastened to calm him. 'OK, you stay there. Can I get you anything?'

'Not at the moment. I've got all I want here.' Brett pulled her closer and rested his head on her shoulder. 'I don't know why you're doing this for me, Laura,' he murmured. 'Why you haven't walked out already I don't know.'

'Because I'm a nurse.'

He raised himself to meet her steady gaze. 'Is that the only reason?'

Laura shook her head. 'I don't think so, but if you don't behave it may well be.'

Smiling, Brett rested his head back on her shoulder and within seconds was asleep.

Laura was reluctant to move and waken him, but she wanted to unpack and check out the kitchen and bedroom. Waiting until she hoped his sleep was sufficiently deep, she slid her shoulder out from under him, gently allowing him to slip further sideways on to a cushion.

He stirred and made himself more comfortable, but he did not waken, so she crept away to inspect the remainder of the flat.

Lifting the bag of provisions his father had thoughtfully brought, she made for the kitchen first. It was small, but appeared to have every labour-saving device imaginable.

Unpacking on to the spotless work surface, she put the perishables into the refrigerator, then filled the kettle and plugged it in. If Brett didn't want a cup of tea, she did.

Leaving the water to boil, she made her way across to what she supposed was the bedroom with the bathroom next door. Pushing open the door, she found the blatant masculinity of Brett's room overpowering. The king-size bed in the centre of the far wall was adorned by a headboard of black trelliswork, which, together with the shiny black bedding, contrasted starkly with the white wall behind. On matching bedside cupboards stood elegant lamps in black and red. Giving an impression of spaciousness, the whole room was reflected in mirrored wadrobes which filled the length of the wall opposite a huge window.

Overwhelmed by Brett's virile personality leaping out at her from the room, Laura was about to carry his case inside when she was struck by the unavailability of anywhere for her to sleep if Brett expected her to stay. Shrugging her shoulders, she completed her task, knowing he must be aware that she had not even a toothbrush with her.

Returning to the kitchen, she made two mugs of tea and carried them over to the black ash coffee-table.

Brett stirred, and for a moment looked at her as if he could not believe his eyes. Then, satisfied, he smiled and reached over to pull her down beside him, and with an unexpected intimacy his lips found hers, at first teasing and tantalising, then hard with a demanding need that left Laura breathless. Her pent-up desire destroying any trace of reticence, she tentatively explored his lips with the tip of her tongue, savouring their piquant firmness.

When at length he gently released her, allowing her to regain her breath, she murmured, 'Brett Farraday, you're a fraud! And your tea's gone cold.'

'What's a cup of tea when I've sampled nectar?' He put his hands on her shoulders, his steady gaze searching her face. 'It worked a treat, didn't it? I thought I might as well use my long years of study to get my own way for once.' He smiled smugly.

Unflinching, Laura returned his scrutiny. 'I was under the impression that you always get your own way.'

'Until I met Sister Pennington.'

Laura's lips compressed a smile as she sensed the warmth of their compatibility for the first time. 'Maybe, and it'll continue that way if you behave as you did last night.'

Brett took her hand in his. 'I'm sorry if I upset you, Laura. Last night I really couldn't help myself, but when I woke this morning feeling so much better, I saw the opportunity I'd been looking for.'

'Don't you be too sure—you'll have to obey my orders, as I'm here as your nurse.'

Brett pulled her to him again. 'Oh, no, that's not my idea at all. I'm fit for anything now.'

'Is that why you exhausted yourself coming home? The moment you sat down you couldn't keep your eyes open.'

'I just needed to unwind, that's all. It's been a harassing morning.'

When Laura did not answer immediately, Brett seized the opportunity to kiss her eyelids, then, leaving a trail of kisses across her cheek, he gently nibbled her earlobe.

'Aren't you taking things rather for granted?' Laura murmured, 'Remember—I came here as your nurse.'

Brett smiled wickedly. 'Mm, but a nurse who told me she loved me only a couple of nights ago.'

She was disconcerted to learn that he remembered her inane ramblings. 'I didn't think you'd recall what I said.'

'I'm fascinated by what my memory took in. I shall certainly be more careful with unconscious patients in the future.' Brett rose stiffly to his feet.

'Would you like me to get you something to eat?' Laura was on her feet behind him, concealing her embarrassment by taking refuge in the suggestion of a commonplace activity.

'No, I'm not hungry. I just want my bed.'

'But. . .' Remembering how he had denied his exhaustion earlier, she was about to argue when the blatant sensuality in his hooded eyes left her in no doubt that it was not sleep he intended.

'Brett,' she was at a loss how to cope with such directness, 'we still hardly know one another.'

'I know I want to spend the rest of my life with you,

so we've wasted enough time already with you playing hard to get.' Brett slung his arm around her waist and tried to urge her in the direction of the bedroom.

'Hard to get?' Laura was indignant. 'You expected me to fall into your arms while you were busy charming every female in the place and taking Marianne's side against me?'

Brett stopped mid-stride and turned her to face him. 'I guessed that was the cause of my unpopularity. Oh, Laura, I was nothing more than a father figure to her. Surely you realised that?'

When Laura didn't answer immediately he bent to cover her lips with his own, murmuring softly, 'What a fool I've been!' As his tongue found her lips and forced them apart to accept his deepening kiss, he pulled her so close that Laura knew he could not miss the pounding of her heart or the hardening of her nipples against his chest.

'Well, are you going to share my bed?' He cradled her hips in his hands, and she experienced the glorious sensation of his masculinity asserting itself.

Moving against him, she whispered, 'I did wonder where you expected me to sleep, but——' Her words were cut short by the force of his mouth on her lips, causing a flood of desire to overwhelm her.

Sensing her helplessness, Brett released her lips, but, keeping a tight hold, opened the bedroom door.

The aggressive aura his personality had stamped on the room soon brought Laura to her senses, but he was too quick for her. Pulling her down to join him on a duvet cover that felt like silk, he raised himself on one elbow, his admiring eyes smiling down at her. 'You're so temptingly beautiful.'

Secure now in the knowledge that he loved her, Laura could not resist teasing him. 'And second only to Marianne.'

'What on earth do you mean? You were never——'

Laura laughed delightedly and laid a finger on his lips to seal his protest inside.

'You always took Marianne's side over our differences of opinion. You——'

It was Brett's turn to silence her protest. 'Surely you didn't think I'd be so unethical as to become involved with one of my patients?' Looking deeply into her eyes, he accused, 'Yes, you did. And all the time I was only trying to help the Barker finances by paying Marianne to do extra typing in the evening.' He chuckled. 'And I suppose the only way I'll ever convince you of my moral principles is to make an honest woman of you before I take you to my bed.' Reluctantly he released his captivating hold, leaving Laura feeling suddenly bereft.

'I'll agree to that only if you marry me as soon as it can be arranged. If you behave this shamelessly with your nurse, it's obviously not safe to let you out of my sight.'

He gathered her into his arms again. 'In that case I'll sack my nurse this minute. I must confess I never could understand why Phil thought her so marvellous, when she obviously disapproved totally of my morality.'

'I——' Intending to disagree, Laura lifted her head indignantly, only to discover Brett's brown eyes laughing down at her.

'You might protest, but I was more than a little envious of the co-operation he successfully wormed from you, while my every request was repulsed. If I hadn't known Phil so well, you could have caused quite a rift between us.'

'I don't know what I'm doing here if you find me such a trial!' Indignantly Laura stirred in his arms.

'Because I like a challenge, and you certainly presented me with one.' Brett's lips lightly caressed her eyelids, her ears and the hollow of her throat. 'You see, I was sure that someone as compassionate as you obviously are must have had a good reason for being as monstrous to me as you were.'

'You. . .' Incensed, Laura struggled out of the circle of his arms, unable to think of anything bad enough to call him.

Brett grinned at her wickedly. 'I know what you're going to say. You thought I was comparing you unfavourably with Sister Jones. Kim told me——'

'Kim? What on earth did she know about it?' Laura was increasingly baffled.

'Only what she heard from Phil. But that was enough for her to realise what a fool I was making of myself.'

'You mean—you mean they knew how you felt before I did?' Laura sighed deeply, then added as an afterthought, 'In fact, it seems everyone knew but me——'

'Oh, no, no,' Brett broke in. 'Not quite everyone. . .'

Recognising the teasing in his voice, she muttered, 'Except your parents and my parents and——' Marianne, she added silently.

Brett tried to appear contrite. 'I couldn't help my feelings being obvious, could I?'

Laura shook her head. 'I must say I did wonder why

your father appeared to expect me to visit you. Seems I must have been blind.'

'No, love, not blind. You just had no time to consider yourself. But not any more. From now on I'll be around to shoulder a share of your problems. Not that there should be any in the future. For a start, you can rest assured that without my disruptive influence at the Wellstead this week everyone will be models of propriety. You can also take time off from worrying about your father, knowing he's in good hands. So I have only one suggestion to make.' Brett's arms closed round her again, as his lips began tasting and caressing her flesh.

'What's that?' murmured Laura innocently.

'Just that we think of no one but ourselves in this breathing-space I've wangled for us. Because the sooner you continue following in Sister Jones's foot-steps the better.' As he spoke, Brett's fingers were feathering lightly up and down her spine.

Though Laura longed to abandon herself to the desire that was swelling within her, she was prevented from doing so by an overwhelming suspicion that her independence was at risk. She sought a respite by catching hold of his wrists. 'You mean give up all I've worked for at the Wellstead?'

'Would you mind so much?' Undeterred, Brett con-tinued his assault on her senses by caressing the delicate shell of her ears with his tongue, then searching out the hollow of her throat with his warm lips.

As Laura arched her back helplessly, he pressed home his advantage. 'I assure you I'm not trying to assume control over your life. I know initially you felt overwhelmed by my lavish lifestyle, but money means absolutely nothing to me without you to share it.' He stroked her cheek gently. 'I mean that sincerely, darling.'

'I realise that, Brett, and I've got you to thank for it.'

'Me?' Brett was puzzled.

'Mm. When you were lying there unconscious I realised that health can't be bought. The only way you were going to recover was by dedicated medical care and skilful nursing. Your financial state was immaterial. Your need was as great as that of the Sudanese you helped. And that's why I'm here. It only took you to need me for me to realise that I couldn't love you more if you were a pauper. Happiness is where the heart is, after all.'

'My sentiments exactly.' After kissing her soundly Brett added, 'However, don't think you're in danger of becoming a kept woman. I do intend you to earn your keep.' He reinforced his teasing by a succession of tantalising caresses.

'How?' Laura murmured between the kisses he was raining on her lips.

'When I suggested you emulate Pat Jones earlier, I was referring to the recent addition to her family. You see, I'm indoctrinated by my mother. I want you to have my children before I'm too old to enjoy them. All right by you?'

'If they're yours, it has to be. Don't you always get your own way?' Laura whispered happily, as she insinuated herself even closer into his embrace, causing them to fall backwards on to the soft black pillows in a happy tangle.

4 MEDICAL ROMANCES AND 2 FREE GIFTS
From Mills & Boon

Capture all the excitement, intrigue and emotion of the busy medical world by accepting four FREE Medical Romances, plus a FREE cuddly teddy and special mystery gift. Then if you choose, go on to enjoy 4 more exciting Medical Romances every month! Send the coupon below at once to:

> **MILLS & BOON READER SERVICE, FREEPOST PO BOX 236, CROYDON, SURREY CR9 9EL.**
> No stamp required

- ✂ - ✂ -

YES! Please rush me my 4 Free Medical Romances and 2 Free Gifts! Please also reserve me a Reader Service Subscription. If I decide to subscribe, I can look forward to receiving 4 Medical Romances every month for just £5.80 delivered direct to my door. Post and packing is free, and there's a free Mills & Boon Newsletter. If I choose not to subscribe I shall write to you within 10 days – I can keep the books and gifts whatever I decide. I can cancel or suspend my subscription at any time. I am over 18.

EP02D

Name (Mr/Mrs/Ms) —————————————————

Address ————————————————————

————————————————————————

———————————————————— Postcode ——————

Signature —————————————————————

— MEDICAL ♥ ROMANCE —

The books for your enjoyment this month are:

A SPECIAL CHALLENGE Judith Ansell
HEART IN CRISIS Lynne Collins
DOCTOR TO THE RESCUE Patricia Robertson
BASE PRINCIPLES Sheila Danton

Treats in store!

Watch next month for the following absorbing stories:

MEDICAL DECISIONS Lisa Cooper
DEADLINE LOVE Judith Worthy
NO TIME FOR ROMANCE Kathleen Farrell
RELATIVE ETHICS Caroline Anderson

Available from Boots, Martins, John Menzies, W.H. Smith and other paperback stockists.

Also available from Reader Service, P.O. Box 236, Thornton Road, Croydon, Surrey CR9 3RU.

Readers in South Africa — write to:
Independent Book Services Pty, Postbag X3010, Randburg, 2125, S. Africa.